MY MR. BEAUTIFUL

ETERNAL CITY LOVE SERIES, BOOK 1

CATERINA PASSARELLI

ISBN 13: 9780692543153
ISBN 10: 0692543155

Covered designed by Najla Qambers Designs

For more, visit www.CaterinaPassarelliBooks.com

"Oh god! Yes! Zack!"

Moaning, the bed thumping against a wall, and screams are coming from my bedroom. Is that *me* moaning out in pleasure?

Nope. I wish.

Would a robber break into my apartment just to have sex? That's kinky enough to be on a reality show.

The moans get louder as I open the door to catch the frisky robbers and my heart stops. Literally, stops beating. Okay not literally, but I'm struggling to take in air.

My boyfriend of a year is riding his redheaded secretary in our bed! You've got to be kidding me.

When they hear me suck in a deep breath, they turn frantically around. They're probably wondering who else was getting sucked on in the room. #Barf

Zack pulls the gray sheet up to cover their naked bodies. He shoots me a look that screams *what the fuck are you doing here?*

I'm home early, not what he expected.

"Elena, baby, I can explain." Zack stumbles out of the bed and awkwardly reaches for his pants.

"Explain?" Tears stream down my cheeks. "Explain what? Why you are fucking someone else in our bed?"

Bolting out of the apartment, Zack chases after me but I make it to the elevator quicker than him.

Watching him trip over his own pants as they slide off his body in the hallway is the last thing I see before the elevator doors close.

What in the actual hell did I just witness?

Zack is a cheater. Add him to the growing list.

————

Now this is what I call living. I drop my leopard luggage off in my new Rome apartment. New to me, at least. This building is centuries old but that doesn't bother me one bit.

It adds to the charm of my new Italian lifestyle. It's entirely different than the apartment I had back home, and that's the reason I know I'm going to love it here.

I guess I can thank Zack for one thing ... giving me the courage to leave Michigan.

Not only is this trip an escape from my breakup, but also a very hectic work life.

I told myself this trip calls for a personal mantra, otherwise I'll revert back to being a big baby in social situations and working myself to the bone.

What's my mantra?

Bold and carefree.

I'm here to be the main character of my own life. This is the exact opposite of who I usually am: an uptight workaholic CEO. Yes, even CEOs get cheated on.

I own the largest social media marketing firm in the United States – Rock Star Media. But the truth is I'm only confident in business. With this trip, I'm about to change that. I left my best friend, Sophie, in charge and booked my one-way ticket.

Staying holed up in this apartment won't allow me to see the sights of the Eternal City, I grab my light black zip up and hit the streets.

The slight chill in the early morning air makes me smile as I walk along the cobblestone streets. They're lined with small cars, houses stacked tall on top of one another, and all the colors of vibrant and bright.

I am no longer in the Motor City.

As I explore, a heavenly chocolate scent floats through the air and blesses my nose. Turning the corner, I see a cute coffee shop, Stella's. Green paint is chipping off the old brick underneath. The caffé sits on a corner next to a pizzeria with an outside patio.

I open the red door and hear a bell chime. The scent of baked goods fills the air. Bookshelves line the walls, small tables and chairs fill the middle of the store, and people are lined up to get the counter. On the large brown marble counter sits what looks like the largest espresso machine I've ever seen.

When it's my turn, a tall man wearing a name tag that says *Marco* greets me.

"*Ciao*! Welcome to Stella's. You must be new here."

"Um, *si*," I say, a little taken aback at his forwardness.

"Sorry." Marco's wide smile reaches his chestnut eyes. "Everyone who walks in here is pretty much a regular. You stood out. What can I get for you?" Marco asks in English with a slight Italian accent.

It took me years of college to learn how to speak Italian and I still can't master their accents.

"Whatever you recommend. Something chocolatey was floating through the air, whatever that is, bring it on." I haven't had anything to eat since the cold, dry Parmesan chicken on my flight from Detroit.

"*Perfecto*! A chocolate biscotto and mocha it is." Marco turns around to get the coffee ready and his shoulders slump. Gone is the chipper facade he greeted me with. When he turns back around, the wrinkles around his tired eyes crinkle. "It's on the house. Welcome to Roma."

"*Grazie!* And they say you guys hate Americans." I tease. "What a wonderful way to be welcomed to the country."

Even though it's not customary to tip in Italy, I'd feel terrible not to. I leave a few dollars for him on the counter.

"Well, that depends on what kind of American we are talking about," he laughs.

I sit down at one of the small tables near the window and bite into my mouthwateringly delicious biscotti. Pulling out my Kindle, I get cozy reading a trashy romance novel. With the buzz of Italians around me, I settle in.

As long as the sexy men stay on the pages of the novels, I'll do just fine in Rome.

2

The warm sunlight peaks into my window and I slowly open my eyes to be startled at the strange room I find myself in. Pinching myself to make sure I'm no longer dreaming, I suddenly remember I'm not in America.

My friends and family thought I was crazy for uprooting myself when my life at home was great. Don't get me wrong. This isn't some kind of quarter life crisis, I guess.

Everything about my days were more of the same and my mind and body craved newness. I was sick of seeing my Facebook Newsfeed full of other 25 year olds and their drama. Add to that the endless hours I was putting in at work and not having a social life whatsoever. This is the change I need.

I throw on a sports tank top, mint green zip up jacket, and Nike leggings. Quickly pulling my long curly brown hair into a high ponytail before I make my way outside. I have no clue where I'm going but I just jog.

About half a mile in, I get my stride and begin to run. New sights, new smells, new people as I pass by. I can't help but to have the cheesiest grin on my face.

After what I estimate is two miles, I turn around and head toward where I hope my apartment should be. Fingers crossed I don't get lost.

A few wrong turns lead me down different paths than my original route. I'm shocked to see I'm back where I was just yesterday.

Stella's.

Maybe it's a sign I should go back for more. What better way to reward yourself after a hard run than to indulge in goodies? #Keep-TellingYourselfThat

The bell dings yet again as I walk into the coffee shop. Marco stands behind the counter looking just as tired as he did yesterday. From personal experience, I can recognize burn out.

When he sees me his face lights up into a welcoming smile.

"You mean to tell me you eat chocolate biscotti every day and keep a figure like that?" He jokes as he gets an espresso ready for me.

"Let's be honest, I run because I love food!"

"So, *come si chiama?*" he asks.

"My name is Elena Scott."

"Nice to meet you, Elena." Marco hands me the espresso.

I pay him and turn to sit down but can't help notice he is the only employee working here. Where is his staff?

"Marco, do you work every day?"

"*Si*, I do. I'm the only one keeping this place afloat."

"Are you the *only* employee here, in general?"

"Yes. Stella was my *Nonna*, and when she passed away," he does a quick sign of the cross, "I decided I would keep the caffé going. Too bad I didn't know it was thousands of dollars in debt."

This didn't take long. I just found my first Italian adventure!

"How about you let me help you?" I step closer to the counter. "I just moved here and I don't have much of a game plan yet. I could help you out around this place."

Marco shakes his head. "That's a really nice offer, but I can't accept your help. I have no way to pay you."

"That's okay." I smile. "I'll do it anyway."

Marco quickly questions my free help, but I assure him my American life allows me to donate my time. I didn't want to let anyone in

Italy know my past but Marco seems to be my first friend, and I can't help but to instantly trust him.

Outside of my bad choices with boyfriends, I'm usually a good judge of people. Let's hope this is a decision I don't regret.

———

A week on the job and I haven't broken anything ... *yet*.

I did, however, spill a latte on an older man. Luckily, for both of us, it was an iced latte. Even though he wasn't burned, no one wants to start their day with cold coffee down the front of their dress shirt. But like Marco first told me, everyone here is a regular. Now the iced latte man, Roberto, jokes about my mishap all the time but continues to leave me tips.

"*Scusi.*" A deep masculine voice, dripping in a sensual Italian accent pulls my head out of the clouds.

Looking up from the counter, my gaze takes in what must be an Italian male model.

For the love of God, I stretch my neck to take in his height as he towers over me. Fighting back the urge to reach over the counter and run my fingers through his thick brown hair, I just stare at him wide-eyed.

He stares back with glistening emerald green eyes that complement his olive skin tone.

Am I drooling?

Holy cannoli. This man is ... beautiful.

There's simply no other word to describe the perfection that is this man.

"*Ciao.*" Mister Beautiful gives me a little wave.

Pull it together, girl. You did not come to Italy for this.

"*Ciao,*" I squeak. Yes, I can now confirm my mouth was hanging open. My cheeks burn with embarrassment. "Welcome to Stella's. What can I *do* to you?"

Mr. Beautiful cocks his head to the side.

My hand flies up to cover my mouth. "I'm sorry. What can I *get* for you?"

7

Did I really just say that?

Though, I must admit there's plenty I'd like to *do* to him, starting with nibbling on his full lips. I've never seen a pair of lips that make me want to instantly run my tongue across them.

"You can *do* anything you want to me." His voice sends heat throughout my already enflamed nerves.

Did I just hear that right? It's not his accent playing tricks with my mind. "What did you say?"

"I said, can I please get an espresso and lemon biscotto?"

Am I living in the Bermuda Triangle? I swear he did not say that. Was he flirting back with me?

"Coming right up!" I turn around to get his drink and cookie.

The entire time I feel his gaze upon me. Normally, I'd be grossed out for someone to openly check me out but I practically eye-fucked him already, I guess we can call it even.

I glance over my shoulder while at the espresso machine and our gazes meet, I quickly turn away before he can see me blush yet again. I need to hurry up with his order as my luck with guys is bad. Cheating secretary boy was just the cherry on top of a large loser sundae.

"Here you go." I put the shot of espresso down on the counter. "That will be five euros."

He hands me 10 euros and tells me to keep the change. I don't have the courage to ask him his name. Mr. Beautiful will have to do.

Watching him leave the coffee shop confirms he's rock solid and muscular everywhere—from his broad shoulders to his tapered waist, and he's got an ass that's cupped tightly in his black dress pants.

Bello e impossibile.

The Italian stereotype of beautiful and out of reach.

As soon as the Italian Beefcake is gone, Marco rushes over to me. My heart is still racing a million miles per minute. I'm grateful no other customers are in line to see me sweat.

"Do you have any idea who that was?" Marco practically gleams with excitement.

If it's possible, I think he's more excited than I am and I'm still wiping up my drool.

"Rome's most eligible bachelor," I jokingly say as I get back to work cleaning off the marble countertops.

"You're right!" He claps his hands together. "And, get this, he's a billionaire!"

I drop the cloth I was holding to the ground.

Did he just say *billionaire*? With a B?

This must be the Universe playing a cruel joke. He's not only the most handsome man I've ever seen, but he's also a billionaire.

How did he make all this money? I've always been fascinated by other business leaders. Not for what's in their bank accounts, because that can be gone in an instant, but for what's inside their minds.

I take off my apron and go to the back room as my shift is over any minute. Marco follows behind me like a puppy with his tail wagging.

"What did he say to you?" he asks.

"Nothing really." I shrug. "I mean, he asked for a lemon biscotto and an espresso."

"I can't believe Leonardo Forte was in Stella's. This is amazing."

"Okay, you are acting like he's the Prince of freakin' England or something. Calm down, Marco. He's just a dude."

"He's not just a *dude*." He mocks my American accent. "He's the closest thing we have to a Prince of Italy. He owns Forte Enterprises, the largest marketing firm in the entire country. He's one of the youngest billionaires in the world. He's also always in the tabloids. Maybe someone will have a picture of him coming out of Stella's."

I might not stay up-to-date on all the latest Italian politics and crime news, but I do have a guilty pleasure for celebrity gossip. Why didn't I recognize him?

"What's he in the tabloids for?" I ask.

"Leonardo is the son of two of Italy's wealthiest families." Marco grabs a broom and sweeps the back room. "But he broke away from his family money and made his own fortune without their help. He's quite a big deal! Plus, he gives so much away to charity and to startup companies with."

"That seems like great news. Why gossip sites then?"

"He dates only the most beautiful women in the world and he frequents through them quickly. He's a legend."

#Heartbreak

And that's where my high hopes drop. Of course a man like that would date only the most beautiful women in the world. Beauty favors beauty.

I'm going to wipe off my drool and forget I've ever seen this guy. Time to clear him from my mind. I did not move to Italy for love, anyway.

Control, alt, delete this encounter away.

"Well I'm glad you got to see your crush, Marco. Maybe next time you can take his order! I'm headed home for the day. I'll see you tomorrow! You can teach me how to make those lemon biscotti."

"Deal!"

3

Marco laughs because I have flour all over myself in my hair, on my white t-shirt and on my green Stella's apron. It's also on the floor, cabinet doors, and counter tops. I am the worst baker on the planet. I may need to stick to making the espressos I'm getting a handle on that. I've even experimented with making my own specialties, and the customers ask for them by name.

Now the baking situation: it's not getting any better. This flour explosion is Exhibit A of why I should stay out of the kitchen.

The bell chimes at the front door but we aren't open yet.

With Marco's hands kneading dough, I'm the one who needs to go handle the early customer. Our regulars should know we technically don't open for another 15 minutes.

And there he is ... Leonardo Forte waiting at the counter.

"Buon giorno. Mi dispiace." Even though my palms are sweating, I'm playing it cool. "We don't open for another 15 minutes, so not all the goodies are out yet. Marco is still hard at work in the kitchen."

"Marco?" he asks, in his deep, rich, Italian accent.

"The owner of Stella's. He's the one responsible for all the magic behind this place." I wave my hands around the caffé until I abruptly stop once I realize I must look like a lunatic.

11

"He is a lucky man to work with a woman as beautiful as you all day."

"Flattery won't get you free baked goods." I laugh. Despite wanting to be unaffected by his compliment, I still melt a little inside. It's been way too long since I've been around a man like him. Actually, I don't think I've been around anyone like him. His presence takes up the entire room. "What can I get for you, *signor?*"

I make sure to say every word clearly this time.

"I'll take an espresso."

I get his drink and let him know it's on the house. Marco would insist if he weren't busy cleaning up my mess.

"Grazie," he says. Then, as we stand across the counter from one another, he leans in ever so slowly that I think he's going in for a kiss. I don't move away as he brushes his hand across my cheek. "You had flour on your face."

"Oh, thank you." I touch my cheek. "I'm the worst baker in Rome."

Hence Marco putting the room back to its normal state.

Leonardo laughs. "What should I call you beside 'Worst Baker'?"

"Worst Baker is fine, but I also answer to Elena."

"Elena...?"

"Elena Scott."

"It's nice to meet you, Elena Scott," he says, extending his hand.

Reaching across the counter to slip my hand into his firm grasp to shake, warmth radiates throughout me in such a blissful way from his sizzling touch. Lingering for much too long with our hands together, I swear time freezes in this moment.

Taking my hand back, I force myself to look away for a moment of composure.

"It's nice to meet you too, Mr. Forte."

"You know who I am?" Leonardo smirks. "I didn't think many Americans follow Italian news."

"How do you know I'm American?" As if my own accent doesn't scream I'm from the Midwest.

"Your charm." Leonardo's devilish smirk captivates me.

"What does that mean?" I bite my bottom lip and his eyes instantly dart there. "Are you being sarcastic?"

He laughs. That must be my winning charm again.

Leonardo downs his shot of espresso and pushes the small cup back toward me. "I don't make many jokes."

"What do you do then?" I pick up his cup and place it in the bin of dirty dishes under the counter.

"For work or ...?"

We let that *or* linger in the air for a moment between us.

"Yes." I push a piece of hair that fell out of my ponytail behind my ear. "For work."

"I'm in marketing. Do you work in the coffee industry back at home too?"

I love how he made me being a barista something that feels much larger; part of the coffee industry.

"No." I shake my head. "How did you get into marketing?"

Leonardo's phone vibrates in his hand. He glances down at it and then back up to me. "Everyone has a story but most people don't know how to tell it. At least not in a way that sells. I want to be the person to help them."

I nod. That's exactly how I feel too but I don't say it.

His phone vibrates a few more times and from where I'm standing I can see numerous notifications lighting up the screen.

"You're a busy man," I say.

Too busy to stand around a coffee shop talking to the likes of me.

He shrugs and places his phone in his jacket pocket. "I seem to be in high demand. A lot of people want something from me."

I can't tell if that was a sexual innuendo or him expressing the true reality of what it's like to run a business.

Everyone does want something from you and it's extremely hard to know if that's a good or a bad thing.

"You shouldn't keep them waiting," I nod to the front door. "And I should switch the open sign on before the regulars barrel through."

"Until we meet again, Elena." He nods in my direction and turns to leave.

Yet again, I admire his hot ass as he walks to the door.

Mr. Beautiful hits the gym, that's for sure.

Leonardo turns back to say something but catches me staring and smirks. "Have a great day."

When he's gone, I immediately sigh. I didn't realize I was holding my breath. I am going to have to maintain better composure if I plan to stick around the coffee shop.

This guy is going to get me into more trouble than I can handle.

———

Pain radiates through my shins and feet. I don't think I've stood this many hours straight in my entire life. Not even when I worked as a waitress in college.

Stella's is really giving me a run for my money.

Even though the idea of staying inside in a warm bath all day sounds appealing, I can't let my first day off since starting at the coffee shop go to waste. I'm ready to explore Rome!

I throw on a pair of skinny jeans, brown riding boots, and a purple button up blouse. I leave my curly hair down; it's a change from always keeping it tied up for work.

On my way out of the apartment complex, I wave to my neighbor in the hall. She's a small older woman who walks with a hunch who reminds me of my own grandmother.

Just like with my trip in general, I don't have a plan for today. Let's see where the city takes me.

The Colosseum is the most obvious place to start as it's one of the most iconic features in the world. After waiting in line for what feels like an eternity, I enter one of history's finest wonders.

Has Leonardo been here?

That's a stupid thought. I'm sure all Italians have.

After spending an hour exploring the Colosseum, I head over to a bar tucked away from the tourist trap for a quick lunch. As I chow down on my four cheese pizza, I spot a tabloid paper on the empty table next to me.

Taking four years of Italian lessons in college makes reading this rag mag much easier. The front page is pure stereotypical with four housewives of Roma and their voluminous black hair, short dresses,

14

and stilettos. I have yet to see anyone like this walking the streets of Rome.

I turn to the second page and there he is. It's like he's lurking behind every corner waiting for me.

"Roma's Most Eligible Bachelor Dates Supermodel
Aurora Rossi"

She's tall with perfect olive skin, perfect white teeth, and a perfect slim body ... perfect everything. I bet he calls her b*ella* while she rides him in bed. I'm going to throw up. Aurora Rossi, you drop dead gorgeous bitch. #Hater

It pains me to throw a world class pizza into the trash, but I no longer have an appetite.

It's late in the afternoon now and tourists are filling up the streets as I walk in the direction of the Trevi Fountain.

I pass a collection of men shouting to buy their stolen purses which they display atop blankets. They'll quickly scoop them up if the police are near. Luckily, they let me pass today without trying to sell me anything. I must look like a woman on a mission.

Hearing the sounds of water, I must be close. I stumble upon the iconic fountain which is jam packed with tourists. Deciding I still want to get closer, I squeeze my way down the few steps to the fountain. Picking a less crowded spot to stand, I dig in my black leather purse for a coin to toss into the water.

As I'm ruffling through the bottomless pit, a young happy couple stands beside me. They're holding hands and can't stop kissing each other. Of course they'd decide to stand next to the single girl with the eternal bad luck when it comes to love.

Found it!

I pick up a coin, turn around, think long and hard about my wish for my company's success, and toss it into the fountain over my shoulder.

I wish for true unconditional love and a happy marriage!

Mind, are you playing games with me? That wasn't the wish we had decided upon before I threw in the coin. When did I become this girl?

15

Throwing coins in a fountain wishing for love. Next I'm going to say I want world peace.

The couple next to me giggles between locking lips. Before I puke, I decide it's time to head back to the apartment.

Approaching my street, I spot a limo taking up all the room in the narrow path. It definitely stands out in my quiet, tucked away neighborhood.

Before I skirt myself around this monstrosity, I hear, "*Ciao, bella,*" from behind me.

I normally ignore dudes catcalling but this limo has got me curious. I turn around, and it's like my own version of Carrie's Mr. Big from *Sex and the City* as Leonardo rolls down the limo window.

"Is that what you call all the girls?" I sass.

"What are you doing? Let's go for a ride." He opens the back door.

A hot billionaire wants to hang out with me. I'd pinch myself again but if I keep doing that I'll surely leave bruises.

"I don't really know you," I say. "How can I trust you aren't looking to kidnap me? I've seen *Taken*. I know how this works."

"You can't be serious." Leo throws his head back to laugh. "I promise I am the Liam Neeson of this movie. You don't need to be worried. But it is wise of you to always be on the lookout while you're here."

"That's easy for you to say." My mother would kill me if she found out what I'm about to do. I slide into the backseat of the limo, hoping that this ends up nothing like the thriller movie. "How did you know where I lived?"

"I went to Stella's to see you and Marco said it was your day off. I wanted to know if you'd like to spend it with me, so I may have convinced him to tell me where you live."

My jaw drops. My boss gave out my personal information?

"I'm going to have to talk to Marco about this. You could be a lunatic!"

As the limo leaves the narrow street, my thoughts drift away from yelling at Marco to the close proximity of Leonardo to me. This is the closest we've been as I'm sitting right next to him. His masculine scent is a light mix of leather and clean soap. Everything about him draws me in.

He's wearing a blue and gray pinstripe three piece business suit. I'd bet lurking underneath is the body of a fitness model.

"How was your day?" He takes off his suit jacket to roll up his dress shirt sleeves, exposing his muscular forearms.

"Lovely." I fidget in the seat and try not to make it too noticeable that I've been checking him out. "I went sightseeing."

"Are you nervous?" Yes, he certainly notices my awkward fidgeting.

"Wouldn't you be?" I tell the truth. "Even though you say you are Liam Neeson, you're practically a stranger to me."

The limo looks like it's circling the city, but I don't have much time to notice our surroundings. The next thing I know, Leonardo's hand grabs mine. Instantly, my skin heats up.

"Bella, are you seeing anyone?"

The serial supermodel dater wants to know if I'm seeing anyone. He's clearly seeing a lot of someones according to the article I read at lunch. I'm not looking to be just another notch in a bedpost of womanizer.

"That's a little forward, even for an Italian." I gently pull my hand back. Not that I don't want him to touch me, I just can't think straight when he does.

"You have experience with other Italians?" he smirks a shit eating grin at me.

He knows I don't.

"Maybe I do, maybe I don't." I shrug and wink.

Where did this confidence come from? I've never been the assertive one or the flirty type before.

Leonardo turns in his seat to face me. "You want to remain mysterious. I can let this slide ... for now. But I predict soon you'll be telling me your every desire. I will be your one and only Italian."

I let out a loud laugh. "You are too much. That was the corniest line ever."

As much as I want to tell him to fuck off, I am curious what it would be like to have him as my one and only Italian. Can I really do something like that? Have a fling with a stranger?

"Can I be a little forward with you again?" He asks.

Turning in my seat to angle my body toward him. "I guess."

Forward is the opposite of what I'm used to. Weasels lying right to my face is the norm.

"Elena," the way he says my name makes me hang on every word, "you are going to love it when we fuck."

"I, uh, I." My jaw drops. I'm at a lose for words. I thought for sure dirty talk would gross me out, but it's surprisingly working for me. Did my panties just get a little wet? "Why are you so confident about this?"

"I am going to find out if those cherry red lips taste as sweet as they look."

"Leonardo, I hope you don't mind me calling you that. It's cute you think you can speak to me like this, but it won't work." It's a bold faced lie that his words are turning me on but I don't want him to know that ... so soon. "Also, I'm not sure if you noticed, but I'm not your type."

"What do you know about *my type?*"

From the rearview mirror, I see the eyes of the limo driver perk up. He cranes his head a bit to the right to listen.

I fiddle with my fingers in my lap. "Well, the tabloids show you love to date supermodels. I, however, am not one of them. I work in a coffee shop, I'm about five six and, as much as I would like to try, I love food too much to be a rail thin model. You will not see this girl strutting on any runways."

His emerald gaze goes from my hands to my eyes. The most intense smolder I've ever witnessed. "You don't realize just how captivating you truly are."

Before I can laugh in his face, he leans in closer to me. It's as if all the air in the limo is vacuum sealed out. I should divert my gaze from his mouth but I can't help to stare.

The next thing I know, his mouth claims mine in the most lusciously slow and delicious kiss. Running my tongue along his bottom lip invites him to put his inside my mouth.

What started off slow and sensual quickly turns passionate and intense.

I run my fingers through his thick hair and tug hard.

What is taking over me? I can't keep my hands off him.

I'm the nice, good girl. I do not make out with strangers in the back of limos.

"We need to stop!" I can barely make myself say the words.

Am I crazy? This feels entirely too good to stop but we have to before I let this go too far.

If it goes beyond a kiss, I will regret it.

Leonardo wipes his mouth and I scoot a little farther away from him toward the limo window. I hope the distance can help me clear my spinning head.

He stays quiet, but his emerald eyes shine at me. He knows he's got me right where he wants me.

"We shouldn't have done that. I don't even know you."

"You keep emphasizing that, but to me, it feels like I've known you my whole life."

I don't say the words but I silently agree. It's as if from the moment he walked into Stella's, he was meant to be in my life.

"I need to focus on my job while here in Rome, not on making out with boys."

Leonardo laughs. "We can stop ... for now. You know you are going to be mine. I know you want me too, Elena."

"You might have been able to get the things you wanted in the past easily, but I am not that easy to get."

"I'm not afraid of hard work," he says, straightening out his light blue dress shirt.

The limo driver pulls up to my apartment complex yet again. I have never before been more excited to get out of a fancy limo and away from an extremely hot guy. The limo barely comes to a stop before I swing the door open.

"I'll see you tomorrow," Leonardo says.

I jump out of the limo and run inside at lightning speed.

What just happened?

And how is he going to see me tomorrow?

4

My phone's alarm clock rings loudly that I jolt out of bed. Getting ready for the day, I can't help but to question this grin I can't get off my face.

That toe curling kiss!

The scent of Leonardo's cologne lingers on my skin. I didn't have the energy to shower last night after I finished myself off with my trusty vibrator thinking of what would have happened if I didn't pull away from him.

But getting myself into yet another heartbreak was not the plan for Rome. No. I need to hit something ... and hard. Looking on my phone's map for the nearest gym, I find one not too far away from my apartment.

The gym looks like it's mom and pop owned, nothing too big or fancy: a row of cardio machines, two group exercise rooms, some punching bags, and more free weights than I can count. The walls are pretty much bare except for mirrors and an occasional motivational poster that looks like it's collected dust.

I appreciate the simplicity, no juice bars or personal trainers hyped up on Red Bull chasing after people.

After signing up for a three month pass, I leave my bag in the locker room. It looks like a kickboxing class is about to begin. I stand toward the back and wait to get started.

A tall, toned blonde instructor walks in wearing a headset microphone to greet the class. She starts the music, and we begin to warm up. As the music blares and our punches fly, I let my body do it's thing. All the tension I've built up since meeting Leonardo eases away, and I am transmitted to another place. This is my element.

Back in the states, I taught group exercise classes to put myself through college when I wasn't working double shifts as a waitress.

The sweat pours from my body but I don't ease up. I will be sore tomorrow. I'm sexually frustrated after my short time with Leonardo and leaving all those emotions in this room feels right.

When class ends, I take a minute to sit on the floor quietly with my eyes closed to meditate.

"*Sei veramente bravo,*" the instructor says as she makes her way to me.

"*Grazie.*" I thank her for the compliment on my job well done.

"Are you *Americana?*"

"Is there a sign on my forehead or something?" I laugh. Just like Marco and Leonardo, she knows I don't belong here.

"I'm not sure I understand?" She laughs but looks a little confused.

"*Mi dispiace.*" I shake my head. "I keep being greeted with the same question about being American."

"Are you staying in Roma? I see you signed up for a three month pass."

My instructor and I walk out of the group exercise room together. I let her know where I'm staying in Rome and that I will be here until who knows when. I did not book a return trip ticket. She doesn't question my sanity, which I appreciate.

I find out her name is Alessandra Palmetto and she's an aspiring model. She grew up in a small town about 45 minutes outside of Rome and moved here after high school.

"I'm going out with some friends tonight for my birthday. You should come!"

Since Marco and Leonardo are the only people I know so far, I happily agree to go to her party and jot down the information in my iPhone.

As much as I want to be excited for my first real plans in Italy, it's time to head to work.

————

"Hey, boss! Off in a hurry?" I joke.

Marco, the hardest working man I know, can surely leave when his shift ends.

"No. *Mi dispiace,* Elena. I have an appointment with the bank in 30 minutes."

"Are you ready? Do you want to role play some questions with me or something? Tell me how I can help you."

"You are too kind. You are doing more than enough to help with Stella's, my *nonna* would have loved you!" Marco puts a manila folder under this arm. "Wish me luck and take care of my baby while I'm at this life changing meeting."

"Buona fortuna."

After Marco leaves I get down to work. Three or four customers enjoy their afternoon espresso as I clean up around the coffee shop. I want this place to look spotless when Marco gets back.

As I'm cleaning the espresso machine, there's a twinge of electricity buzzing in my body. How is it that I haven't seen his face yet my body is on fire? Leonardo is here. It's as if we share some kind of energetic connection.

I compose myself before turning around. I don't want him to see how much I want him because I'm sure my need is written all over my face.

"You missed a spot." He points to the machine.

"Ha ha," I mock. "I thought only Americans had corny dad jokes like that." That gets a laugh out of him, a deep, sexy laugh. "What can I get for you, sir?"

His eyes widen after I call him sir. Did I just catch Leonardo off guard? One point for me. He quickly stands a little straighter, wiping the smirk off his face.

"I'll take whatever you recommend."

After I make his caffé *Americano* he takes a seat at one of the small tables near the back bookshelves and pulls out a laptop. Looks like he's making himself comfy today.

I wait on a few more customers and, when no one else is in line, I head over to Leonardo's table, bringing him a chocolate raspberry biscotto that Marco made before he left.

He looks up at me with his emerald eyes, surprised. "*Grazie*. Are you taking a break?" he asks while I take a seat at his table.

"When the boss is away, the employee will play." I laugh and scan the coffee shop to make sure everyone looks taken care of.

"I could think of a few fun ways to play."

And just like that, my pussy quivers. How does he do this to me every time? It's the way he growls his dirty phrases at me with that accent.

"None of that in my workplace, sir." I point to his laptop. "What are you working on?"

"Just some boring proposals I need to review before a conference tomorrow morning."

"Don't you have a big fancy office somewhere you can review them at?"

"Of course I do, except I like it here better. The company is rather beautiful."

"I'll let the other customers know you think they are beautiful." I laugh at compliment to keep me from blushing. "So what's the conference about?"

Leonardo looks deeply into my eyes before explaining the intricacies of his proposal. With each passionate word, I see how he wins his business deals. He's the beauty *and* the brains.

"We are looking to expand into teaching dentists how to market their businesses on the Internet. It's a new venture after working with so many other types of business and brands. Dentists here tend to be, how do you say *vecchia scuola* ... old school in the way they market their businesses."

"Can I see your proposal?"

My business senses flare up excitedly. I haven't worked on a project

23

since before I decided to ditch the States, and I try to remind myself not to let it show.

You are taking a break, Elena.

"Are you interested in marketing?" He turns his laptop in my direction.

It touches me that he's willing to share his work. My former self would never have given a glimpse into her working world. Before I can answer his lingering question, I notice a customer approach the counter so I excuse myself and get back to work.

"Ciao, signora Lucca! Can I get you your usual?"

"Si." She nods her head.

I love chitchatting with her while I make her coffee. Signora Lucca is in her fifties and has three adult children who all live outside of Roma. I think she needs our daily interactions as much as I do.

She leans over the counter as I ring her up. "Elena, you have to meet my doctor. You two would make a great pair!" Before I can cut her off, she continues. "He's tall, smart, handsome, and extremely kind. I hope you don't mind," she fiddles with the cup I gave her, "but I told him he to call the caffé and ask for you. His name's Carlo."

I can't believe that my customer is trying to hook me up.

"Grazie, signora Lucca." I muster up a fake smile. "I just don't think I'm ready to date. I'm just settling in Rome."

She waves her hands around in the air. "Honey, there is never a time when a beautiful woman like yourself is not ready to date." She laughs. "I'm just worried that Marco has you working too much and you aren't allowing yourself time to enjoy the city! If I were your age, I'd be out with a different guy every night." She shimmies her chest. "Enjoy life while you are young."

Is Signora Lucca trying to get me laid?

"Don't worry, *signora*, I'm going out to a party tonight."

She claps her hands together and smiles. *"Bella!* I'm happy to hear that. And don't forget to thank me when you meet Carlo." She heads out of the caffé with her drink in hand.

I shake my head and laugh. Even though I'd rather not have my number passed around, I can't help but to be touched that she's looking out for me.

With the line now empty, I clean off the counters and sweep the floors until I notice Leonardo is the only customer left in the building.

I make eyes at him before heading to the back room to put the cleaning supplies away in the closet. From inside this tight space, heat radiates behind me.

"Where are you going tonight, *cara?*" he whispers into my ear as he brushes my hair aside.

"I, uh, have a birthday party to go to for a new friend," I say with my back still turned to him.

I can't concentrate with him standing behind me like this. And I most definitely can't let this get out of hand like in the limo. What I told *Signora* Lucca was correct.

I'm not ready to date anyone.

He nuzzles his nose into my neck as I tilt it to the side inviting him in. Did he just smell my hair?

And didn't I just tell myself not to do this?

"Is this friend a girl ... or a guy?" he gently licks my neck.

My brain feels like it's on a rollercoaster. His lick sparked untapped passion lingering within my core. Leaning back into his buff chest, I whimper. With one lick he has me falling apart.

"Answer me." He runs his fingertips up my arms. Goose bumps break out across my body.

"A woman," I whisper back.

Ever so slowly, he brings his mouth to my exposed neck and sucks. My body overrides any coherent thought in my brain.

To hell with all that stupid shit I said about not wanting to let this go any farther.

With Leonardo behind me, I wrap my arm around the back of his head, running my fingers through his thick hair. He brings his body firm against mine and his massive erection presses into my back.

"I love the way your body reacts to me," Leonardo says.

Before I can reply, he spins me around. My back knocks into the wall of the closet and Leonardo cages me in. His hands rest on the wall on both sides of my head.

Reaching out, I pull him by his dress shirt into me. Our mouths collide feverishly—hot and heavy are our kisses.

25

He sucks on my bottom lip and I run my fingers down his chest. I wish this shirt was not preventing me from clawing his bare skin. Marking him as my own.

Leonardo removes one hand from the wall to run it over the front of my shirt, stopping to grab my breast. My nipples go hard.

My body react likes it's never been touched before. #Traitor

Deciding now is the time to be bold, I reach for his pants and pull on the zipper, but he grabs my hand.

"Not yet," he whispers.

Why stop? He seems to be just as affected as I am.

"What's the matter?" My body was all too willing to give myself over to him in this very moment. To throw caution to the wind.

"This isn't where we are going to fuck for the first time." Leonardo pulls us apart. "I don't want it to be in a cleaning supply closet. You deserve better than that."

"Oh really?" My hands land on my hips. "Who put you in charge?"

The mood ends. I'm touched he wants to give me more, but my horniness upsets me. I'm also a little crushed that he has the ability to resist me.

The heat evaporates from the supply closet and leaves me with a slight chill.

We straighten up our clothes and leave the storage closet together. I can't even think straight, and I stumble into a table leg outside the door. He catches me and holds me to his muscular chest.

"How am I supposed to trust you out on the streets of Rome by yourself? You can't even walk in this caffè."

"It's not my fault you make me feel loopy. Stop judging. And I'm a big girl, I can handle myself well on my own."

"I'll be the judge of that." He chuckles as he lets me go.

We walk out the front door as I lock up. On the front step, we stare at each other awkwardly, neither knowing how to say goodbye.

"Thanks for stopping by today. I'm sure Marco will be happy to hear you like his *nonna's* coffee shop."

"Marco, huh? And *you* aren't glad I stopped by, too?"

"Don't push your luck."

"Have fun at your party tonight. Don't do anything I wouldn't do."

26

"So, no sex?" I smirk.

His eyes go wide.

Two points for Elena.

"If you are having sex with other people, then we are done here."

Did he really just give me some kind of ultimatum? How dare he! We aren't dating. And how do I know he's not having sex with other people? What about the models? He could run out of here right now and have some chick waiting at his place to fuck.

"Whatever you say, captain." I give him an awkward salute. "I'll be sure to keep it in my pants ... that is, if I even want to end up having sex with you anyway."

I hop off the step and walk in the direction of my apartment. He doesn't chase after me, and I don't look back.

5

"Damn, girl, you look good!" Alessandra says when I walk into the club. I'm wearing a skintight black dress that stops just above the knee. There's lace around the collar, and I paired it with gold, open toed high heels. It has to be the most daring outfit I brought with me to Rome.

This place with its dim lights and bumping music definitely has nightlife! Private rooms hidden behind curtains sit at the corners of the bar, high tables for dancing dot the center of the room, and shirt-less bartenders pour drinks. From the ceiling, women perform acrobatic tricks on silk ropes.

"*Grazie*! You, too, birthday girl!" I shout over the music. Alessandra would make a frock look elegant, but she's wearing a sexy little low cut black dress that's covered in sequins.

Alessandra introduces me to her friends—three brunettes, a redhead, and a blonde. They smile at me nicely but it's too hard to hear them over the music.

I grab a cherry vodka with sugar free Red Bull from a strapping young Italian at the bar and then head back to where the girls are now dancing on the high tables. I climb up, proud of myself for not spilling my drink, and let go to the music.

Just like I love to kick box, I love to dance. Outside of exercise and dance, my body doesn't feel like it's my own. Tension normally runs through my muscles and physical touch isn't the first thing I gravitate toward.

But when I dance all the emotions come out.

Three cherry vodkas and one shot of tequila in honor of the birthday girl later and my body is buzzing.

As a lightweight, I never drink this much. But I don't care. I'm covered in sweat, can't feel my feet, and I'll probably go deaf after tonight, but I'm having a great time with my new friends.

When it's time to call a cab, I try to settle my tab with the bartender but he let's me know it's already been taken care of. When I try to dispute him, he nods his head in the direction of one of the secluded curtained off areas of the club.

Curiosity wins over sensibility as I walk toward the area and pull back the black curtain. Sitting on a dark red couch looking down at his smartphone is Leo.

"What the heck are you doing here, *Leo*?" I say, testing out the new name. I stumble onto the couch, noticing he's the only person in this room.

"Leo?" He puts his phone in his pocket. "No one calls me that."

"Well ... I'm not 'no one'," I say, with a new found confidence. Or liquid courage.

"*Si,* you definitely are not 'no one.' You look like you are having a good time."

"Have you been watching me all night? How did you know I was at this club?" My head's spinning slows down a bit. "This is kind of creepy, dude."

"I have my ways ... *dude.*" He knows I will not accept that bland answer as I stare at him. "I own this club. I had a last minute meeting with our marketing manager for a commercial we are launching this week. When I was leaving I noticed you shaking your ass on the dance blocks."

Of course he'd own this club. I remind myself I need to Google him later. What else does he own? All of Rome?

Leo distracts me by picking up my feet and unbuckling the straps on my heels. He takes my right foot into his hands and rubs.

Oh, my God.

It's like I've died and gone to heaven. I let out a small moan.

"Are you enjoying this?" Leo lifts my left foot to his mouth and slowly kisses up my leg. He makes his way to my knee and then nibbles on my upper thigh.

"Yes." The word escapes me before I can pull it back in.

"Do you want this?" he asks, as I notice his voice is a little hoarse.

"Yes," I growl, distracted by his nearness to my pussy. Our sexual tension is so thick in the air between us. Get on with it already, man.

"We aren't going to have sex tonight." He puts my leg down on the couch, and in a second, his face is in between my thighs. "Do you understand?"

If this is just like the cleaning supply closet again, I don't want it. "Why not?" I whisper.

"You are too drunk for that."

"No, I'm not." I sit up straighter on the couch. "It's been hours since my last alcoholic beverage."

"Elena," he pushes my dress up over my waist, "Don't worry, I'll still take care of you."

He moves my lace thong to the side, and before I can think about what he's going to do next, his mouth sucks on my sex. I grab the couch as he slurps at my folds. His tongue is all over me—from my clit to inside my pussy.

"Oh, God, Leo." I arch my back as I fist a pillow by my side.

He looks up at me from between my legs with a devilish grin. Seeing his face in-between my thighs turns me on even more. Truthfully, I find this to be more erotic than penetration.

When I don't think the sight can be any more glorious, he sticks a finger inside of me as his hot tongue circles my bud. I grind myself into him—fucking his handsome face.

Leo sticks another finger inside and bites down on my inner thigh.

Closing my eyes, I let Leo work his tongue and fingers around my pussy—worshipping me like a feminine goddess. No man has ever taken this much time to bring me to arousal.

When my legs quiver, I slam my thighs hard around the sides of his head.

He bites my clit, and I nearly scream. Having to pick up the pillow and cover my face before I do it again. However, Leo quickly pulls it away from me.

"Don't cover yourself. I want to hear you," Leo says.

He curls his expert fingers inside my sex and hits my G spot. The tightness throughout my body melts away as the intensity pushes me to new heights.

This is it! My orgasm explodes out of me and I pant as my body quakes upon release.

For the first time since I've walked behind the curtain, I remember that we are in a public place.

I have never done anything like this before and instantly I'm embarrassed. This woman I've become since landing in Italy is entirely different from the one I am at home. Yet, I keep making this remark. Maybe this version of me has laid dormant inside for years, waiting for the right time to make herself known.

Wild, untamed, and free.

I don't have long to consider what this means as my eyelids grow heavy.

I pass out blissfully.

———

My head weighs 100 pounds. Dear God, are needles stabbing my brain? What the hell happened last night? I have never gotten drunk enough to black out before. I swear I did not come to Italy to be reckless. Yes, I want to have fun but that was a little much. I need to get a hold of myself.

It's not until I open my eyes that I see I'm not even in my own apartment. Instead, I'm in the biggest bedroom I've ever seen. It's got a gothic feel with black and red bed sheets and a King sized mahogany bed that I'm the only person lying in right now.

Pulling down the sheets, I'm still wearing yesterday's little black dress, but my heels lay on the floor near the door.

Am I at Leo's? I sure hope so.

I pull the covers back, grab my heels, and walk to find out just where I am, killer hangover and all.

With my heels in my hand, I walk barefoot down a giant marble staircase and toward what smells like the kitchen.

Unlike the gothic feel in the bedroom, this kitchen is light and airy. Double islands stand in the middle of the room; on one of them sits a bottle of water and two ibuprofen waiting for me.

"Good morning, *bella*," Leo says from behind me.

He's standing in the doorway wearing blue jeans hanging low on his hips, a plain black t-shirt, and bare feet. His hair is wet. From brooding businessman to laid back boy next door, he makes it all look extremely sexy. I can't decide which I like better.

"Your house is amazing."

"*Grazie, bella.*" He pours himself a cup of coffee and sits down at the table right after pulling out a chair for me to join him.

I sit next to him and keep chugging my water. My mouth is drier than the desert.

"So, what happened last night after we ... you know?"

"*You know?*" He picks up the morning paper and skims over it. "Are you afraid to say it, Elena?"

"You know ... after you gave me an orgasm with your tongue. Is that what you wanted to hear?" I'm surprised I'm able to say the words.

He laughs. "You passed out on the couch in the club. I told your friends I was taking you home and then put you to bed."

"My friends let you take me out of the club? They don't even know you. Wow, some friends. I can't believe it!"

First Marco and now Alessandra. What's with these Italians?

"Elena, calm down." He takes my hand into his. "Those women frequent the club and they have met me before. Most people have." He traces circles with his finger on the top of my hand. "My life tends to make it into the gossip magazines and on entertainment news shows. Trust me, they know who I am. They did not send you off with some stranger."

I hope that's the case. Whenever I'm with Leo, it feels like just the two of us, but all of Italy must be watching him.

I'm sitting at the kitchen table wearing last night's dress with the country's most eligible bachelor billionaire.

Do I want this? My heart has been broken far too many times. I can't seem to keep a man or make one happy. I know a man like Leo, a serial dater who can get anyone he wants, wouldn't want anything longterm.

I certainly don't want to waste anyone's time. I should just end this before it goes any further. Pulling our hands apart, I get up from the table and walk to the front door all in a matter of seconds.

"Where are you going?" Leo runs behind me.

"I should go home now." I slip my shoes on. "I've overstayed my welcome."

"I wouldn't say that. You are welcome to stay as long as you wish." His eyes search mine for any hint of what just happened.

"No, thank you. I've got a life to get back to." I walk out the front door and slam it shut behind me.

Again, he doesn't chase me.

Do I want him to?

Why am I so confused about what I want?

When I get outside, I have no idea where I am. It looks like we are in the countryside. A wrought iron gate stands at the end of a circular driveway, gorgeous purple Wisteria flowers drape the walls and gates, and there's even a water fountain in the middle of the driveway covered in moss.

I get out my iPhone, take a photo of the view, and then ask Siri to look for a cab service before a black town car pulls up in front of me.

The older man who was with Leo when he picked me up at my apartment the other day rolls down the window and tells me he will take me home. Now, normally, I wouldn't get in a car with a stranger, well at least not twice in the matter of a few days, but I don't know where the heck I am or how much a taxi ride will be. Plus I seem to be breaking all the rules I've set for myself since landing in Italy.

I climb into the backseat. The glass divider is down, and I take the time to study the driver: he's tall with silver white hair, a mustache, and black framed glasses. His broad shoulders are in perfect posture.

"I don't even know your name." I break the awkward silence.

"My name is Mateo, *Elena*." He puts an emphasis on my name to let me know that he knows exactly who I am.

"Thanks for driving me home. I appreciate the offer."

"I would love to say the idea was my own. I would never make a lady walk or, worse, take a taxi, but my boss is very gracious. It was his idea."

"Yeah, what a guy." I chuckle.

"You'd be surprised." He switches his eyeglasses to a dark pair of sunglasses. Great, now I can't read his expression in the rearview mirror.

"Where are we?" I glance out the window at the picturesque landscape.

"We are in Tivoli, just outside of Rome. *Signor* Forte has an apartment in the city close to his headquarters, and then he has this place, which is, as you say in America, his pride and joy, plus a few other places."

Staring out the window, I take in as much of the sights of Italy as I can until I nod off into a nap.

Hangovers suck.

Italian men suck too.

They sure do.

————

"Signorina Scott," Mateo gently says. "We're to your apartment now." He stops the town car in front of my building.

"Grazie, signor."

"No need to thank me." He smiles and opens the door for me.

As I'm walking toward the main door to my building, I swear I hear Mateo mumble something under his breath.

"Scusi. I didn't catch that?"

Mateo removes his sunglasses. "Don't judge him too quickly. Signor Forte gives the ones he loves the world."

I stare back in shock. Is the driver really giving me dating advice? First, Signora Lucca and now Mateo. That's how bad my life is right now.

"I'm sorry, it's not my place to talk," he adds after he sees my surprised expression.

"That's okay!" I laugh. "Dating advice keeps coming my way."

It must be obvious that I have absolutely no clue what I'm doing.

Mateo nods and gets on his way.

When I'm back in my apartment, I shower off the club smell from yesterday and contemplate how I got myself here.

This is what happens when you don't have a plan.

6

Hashtags, algorithms, and revenues—these things come easy to me. I excel at marketing, branding, and leading other people into action.

But making coffee and Italian baked goods? This has taken me more time to pick up than I'd like to admit.

Monday morning rolled around and I came into Stella's with fresh dedication and excitement for my role here. No longer will I chase after Italian men or party like I'm a freaking rock star on high top tables.

That wild woman is going back to the cave she's been living in.

Waiting for my first customer, I stand at the counter and daydream about my family. I miss them. The last time I spoke to my mom she told me she and my dad were planning a vacation to Florida. This reminds me of being a kid, when our family would load up into the minivan and drive 24 hours from Michigan to Florida each and every summer. I give my parents credit for surviving being trapped in a van with three kids for so long. #Troopers

The daydream quickly ends when the bell chimes as my first customer enters. Time to get to work.

Italians are quick when it comes to their coffee.

Order, take their espresso shots, leave. Rinse and repeat.

No lingering in the morning for the most part. Hours pass by quickly and I'm finally in the groove. If my interns could see how well I am fetching coffee, they'd be shocked.

It's until Marco taps me on the shoulder that I glance at the clock and see my shift is over.

"Elena, did you hear the good news?" His smile is wider than I've ever seen it.

"Good news? Can't say I have." I untie my apron. "The only thing I've heard are orders for espresso from a bunch of over caffeinated Italians." I laugh.

"Our most eligible bachelor is in the papers again!"

My heart drops. Another supermodel? Could he have moved on so quickly?

Marco sees I'm looking a little pale and worried. "Are you okay?"

"What's he in the paper for?"

He gives me a once over and then hands me the latest issue of TMZ Italia.

Compose yourself. I take a second to catch my breath and then I look.

Roma's Most Eligible Bachelor Spotted At Local Caffé

Thank sweet baby Jesus! The frog that's been sitting in a bundle of nerves in my throat dissipates.

"We should hang it up and frame it! It's like royalty was hanging out here." Marco cuts the article out of the paper and tacks it to the bulletin board. "This will do for now."

"Are you really going to hang that thing up?"

"Okay, Elena, tell me what this is really about. You looked like you might, as you say in America, 'toss your cookies' when I told you Leonardo was in the paper."

Do I really want to get into my personal life with Marco? This is normally a conversation I'd save to have with my best friend, Sophie, but with the time difference and her taking charge of my company, it's been hard to get a moment to speak with her.

And that's how I find myself spilling the coffee beans to Marco.

37

"Well … we kind of went out the other night, and then I ran out of his house the next morning and haven't heard from him since."

Marco pauses for longer than necessary. What the hell is thinking? That I made a huge mistake? That I'm some kind of floozy? Or airhead? Or …

Finally, he asks, "Why did you leave?"

"Why?" I repeat the question as if the answer were the most obvious thing. "He's Rome's most eligible bachelor, that's why."

"Bachelors usually become husbands. Do you not want to get married?"

"Whoa, whoa." I hold my hands up in front of my chest. "I didn't mean to make this about marriage. I do want to be married, yes. But I'm not sure if Leo would want to settle down … ever."

"So you don't want to date an eligible bachelor *and* you do want to get married *and* Leo has taken you out … what's the problem again?"

"You ask a lot of questions!" I huff.

"Are you avoiding an answer because you don't want to be honest about why you ran off?" #NailedIt

"Fine." My hands go to my hips. "I ran off because I've dated way too many men who are just like him or worse. I don't do well with relationships. I always have the worst luck. If it were to happen this time, then the whole world at least all of Italy, will know and see my failure."

He nods at me. "What else?"

Okay, this man is good. How does he know there's more?

"What if I'm not good enough and can't make him happy?"

Here we go again with another long pause from Marco. What does he think about when he's quiet for so long?

"That's impossible." Marco stares at the article on the wall and then back at me. "Did these past boyfriends make you feel like you weren't special?" #Bingo

I divert my gaze away from Marco's kind face. His interrogation pierces my heart.

"A few." Finally, some honesty. "I didn't date a bunch of guys, but the ones I did … it never ended well. It usually had to do with them either cheating, thinking they could do better than me or because I was 'boring' and always working." I shake my head. "A man like Leo would want someone who is exciting, alluring, and something quick."

That's tough to get out without feeling like an absolute loser.

"The fact that Leonardo came here and, as the papers say, sat here for *hours* working shows he has some kind of interest in you."

"But for how long?"

"That's a great question ... for him. You should ask him."

Without wanting to face anymore brutal honesty, I put my apron in the drawer and grab my purse. "Alright, Mr. Miyagi, thanks for your advice. On that note, I'm heading out now. Enough life lessons for one day."

He laughs as Signora Lucca walks in, and I slip into the backroom before she sees me and quizzes me about her doctor again.

———

Right after work and that intense conversation, I know exactly where I want to go: to clear my head in the gym.

No group exercise classes are starting anytime soon, so I hit the StairMaster. Eminem raps loudly through my headphones as the sweat pours out of my body. I'm halfway through my playlist when I sense his presence.

What is he doing here?

Doesn't he have a high powered job he should be at?

Why the heck is he at the gym in the middle of the day?

And why isn't he at a posh gym, not your regular ol' gym?

If he's going to ignore me, I'm going to do the same.

I towel off after stepping off the machine and cleaning it with disinfecting spray. My songs still play as I turn back to walk toward the machine, and I literally bump into a wall.

A wall of man. Solid muscle on display in his gym shorts and muscle shirt.

Avert your eyes, Elena.

"What are you doing here?" I take out my earbuds to ask.

Even those are sweaty which is disgusting. If Leo didn't think I was below his standards before, he will now.

Supermodels can't possibly sweat.

"I should ask you the same thing. Shouldn't you be working?" Leo smiles as if there isn't awkward tension lingering in the air between us.

"Marco asked me to trade my afternoon shift with his morning one. Something to do with figuring out his new business partner. Shouldn't *you* be working?"

"I go to the gym every day."

That's obvious by the defined cuts in his body.

"This gym? It doesn't seem like your style, not fancy enough."

Leo shakes his head. "No, this is not my regular gym, but I heard it was nice so I wanted to check it out.

"Who told you it was nice?" I quiz him.

Is he stalking me?

"Your friend Alessandra told me when I was at the club with you the other night."

I completely forgot the gym girls were at the club. Okay, maybe he's not here for me then.

Wait ... my stomach aches, is he here for Alessandra? She is an aspiring model, and models are his thing. And she could pass as Aurora WhatsHerFace's cousin.

"So, did you come to see Alessandra? I don't think any group classes are starting until tonight." My glance down at my tennis shoes and then back up to meet Leo's emerald eyes.

"No, I'm not here to see Alessandra. What is this an interrogation?" Leo laughs. "You should have been a cop."

"If I was interrogating you, you'd know it." I walk in the direction of the women's locker room and he stays at my side. "Just trying to figure out why you just so happen to be here at the same time I just so happen to be here."

Leo halts in this step. "*Cara*, I had no idea that you wouldn't be working. I honestly came to see if this gym was worth *owning*. Do you think I would stalk you?" He frowns.

"Well ... if the tennis shoe fits." I wink. As I'm walking into the locker room, he grabs my arm and spins me around to face him.

"Let me make this clear." He steps closer to me. "I do *not* have to stalk a woman to get to know her. The tennis shoe does not fit, you smarty pants."

"Fine." I take a step back. "I get it."

Not that he owes me any explanation after what I just accused him of, he says, "This gym is owned by two guys in their early 20s who are working hard to get it off the ground. I was thinking of investing. We had a meeting this morning and they told me I could use the gym to get a first hand experience."

It makes me happy to hear he is interested in helping out people who are less fortunate.

"Well, I admire that about you." I smile up at him. "And I'm sorry I jumped the gun and made you feel like a creepy stalker."

"It's okay, *cara*. What are you doing when you leave here?"

"I haven't really thought that far ahead. Work, gym, home, repeat. That's pretty much my days since I've been here."

"Have you seen anything outside of Rome?"

"This isn't my first time in Rome. I came on a tour years ago as a teenager. But on this trip so far, no, I haven't ventured outside of the city."

"Would you like to go out with me tonight?"

Do I? I just ran out on him the other day and now I've just accused him of stalking me. And he still wants to go out? My spinning mind is about to explode.

"Honestly, it would be better if we could just remain friends," I say.

How long could Mr. Beautiful be interested in me? I don't want to wait around until he's done with me to find out. Not only would I face rejection but it would be an internationally publicized rejection.

"*Friends?* I have enough friends, Elena. I sure as hell don't want to be your friend." His eyes narrow.

"We can't be friends?" I say, taken back by his brutal honesty.

"No." He shakes his head. "Not friends. I want to be your lover."

Lover? No guy has ever referred to himself as being my lover before. Is this an Italian thing? I don't think I'm cut out to be anyone's lover, it sounds too sexy or grown up. And 'lover' doesn't translate into 'girlfriend' or anything more serious. It means we sleep together and that's it. I've never been anyone's friends with benefits, and I don't want to start now.

"I don't think *lovers* works for me." I glance down, a little embarrassed.

"Elena." Leo tilts my chin up with his fingers to look him in the eyes. "I'll help you see that you want this as much as me."

"Whatever you say, Mr. Beautiful," I say.

I laugh off the serious conversation before breaking away from him and heading into the ladies locker room where I fight back the sudden urge to cry.

7

An explosion of pastries greets me when I walk into the kitchen of Stella's. Marco is slaving away in the kitchen doing what he does best—bake.

"What is going on in here, Pastry King?" I ask.

"You aren't going to believe it! We got a large catering order to deliver pastries and coffees to Forte Enterprises today."

"Do we do catering? And did you say Forte Enterprises?"

"We do catering when someone as high profile as Leonardo Forte wants our baked goods in his office." Marco looks away from his pastry dough long enough to explain his order. "Could you help me box these up? I hope you don't mind but I need you to be the one to deliver these. I have another meeting to get the business partners contract agreement drawn up that we've been talking about."

"Oh yeah, that." I grab a box to put all the cannoli in. "If you need anything more from me about the contracts, let me know. I'm here to help you."

"The best thing you can help me with right now is to take my van and deliver these. Please Elena, I know you don't want to do this, but it would mean so much."

I look into Marco's puppy dog eyes and I know that I have to.

Marco would do anything for me and I need to step it up for Stella's and deliver these baked goodies to Mr. Beautiful.

Once we have all the goodies boxed up, I'm out the door. I haven't had to drive around Rome by myself, always walking or taking taxis but there's a first time for everything

By the time I get to Forte Enterprises, I'm on edge after that scary ride over. I have never seen such crazy drivers, and I actually feared for my life.

Carrying the boxes of pastries, a kind stranger sees me and opens the double glass doors. At the front desk a petite brunette with a short pixie cut wearing black designer glasses sits behind the desk and glances up at me from her computer screen.

"Can I help you?"

"Hi! I'm here from Stella's to deliver the pastries you ordered."

"I wasn't aware of any pastries. Hold on just one minute." Miss Pixie Cut is all business; she promptly picks up the phone and talks in Italian a million miles per minute to someone on the other line. She's speaking so quickly I don't understand her.

"Take the elevator up to the twenty third floor and set them up in conference room B."

Set them up? I thought this would be a simple 'here's your pastries and run' type of delivery. I don't want to question her because she's already back on the phone bossing someone else around.

I stroll over to the elevator and go up to the twenty third floor. When the doors slide open, I find a giant open floor space with floor to ceiling windows. I walk through a waiting room area past white couches and chairs. On a glass coffee table, a few Entrepreneur magazines with Leo's face on the covers lay scattered about.

Yet again, there's another desk and another women gatekeeping it. I ask her where conference room B is located. She questions me just like Pixie did. Why isn't anyone aware of these pastries?

After another phone call, she gives me a once over. Did this secretary just size me up? She's speaking to someone about the pastries when the double doors behind her open and Leo walks out.

My breath hitches at the sight of him. He looks all business, all power, and super sexy. He's wearing a black and white three piece business suit and a ridiculously adorable pair of black glasses. I didn't think this man could draw me in anymore, but he always seems to surprise me

"Elena, come in." Leo motions his hand inside the room.

I hear him mutter something to his secretary which I think means 'hold my calls' as I walk into the room.

It takes me all of two seconds to realize this is not conference room B; instead, this must be Leo's personal office. Just like in the lobby, there are floor-to-ceiling windows showing off the city of Rome, a dark red wood desk, bookshelves, a leather couch, and two chairs on the opposite side of his desk.

"I'm supposed to set this up in conference room B." I lift the pastry boxes a little higher to put some space between us.

"I know, but the conference cannot start without me, so we have a few minutes."

He takes the boxes from my hands and sits them down on a small table near the couch, and he motions for me to take a seat.

I remain standing, trying to keep a professional air about this meeting. I remind myself that I am here to represent Stella's.

"I want to talk to you about the other day, at the gym. I'm sorry if it felt like I ambushed you. I was just as surprised to see you there as you were to see me," he says.

I'm shocked a man like Leo is confident enough to say 'I'm sorry.' The guys in my past never admitted any fault.

"It's okay. My emotions have been all over the place since I got to Rome. I overreacted," I say, trying to avoid this conversation all together.

Why can't he drop this and let me go?

"I want to start fresh with you. You didn't seem to respond well to the idea of being lovers, and I think it's because we don't know each other very well."

Where did that come from?

The truth is, he's right. I don't know him very well, but that's not what was holding me back. I don't want to tell him that it has to do with my past and insecurities.

"Uh, yeah," I mutter. "That's it. We don't know each other very well."

"I'd like to take you on a date. Just two people getting to know each other."

I cock my head to the side. "You mean, like *friends*?" I say the word he freaked out over during our last conversation.

His eyes light up, knowing that I caught him.

"I have never done *friends* before, but for you, I will try something new. I can't promise to give you anything more than lovers though. I hope you realize this."

"You mean you can't do an official relationship as boyfriend and girlfriend?"

"Correct, I do not do relationships." Leo glances out the window for a moment. "I am not suitable to be anyone's long term anything and I, honestly, do not want to be."

I wonder what makes him 'not suitable' to be anyone's boyfriend or husband? I don't want to ask though. Right now, I don't think I'm ready to push him or to hear the answer.

He doesn't come out and say it, but I come to the conclusion he's suggesting we'll start as friends and end up as friends with benefits. I'm not a 'friends with benefits' kind of girl. I know I want a real relationship, but in this moment I don't care. I am so intrigued by this man; I want to get to know him better, however he's going to offer up the chance.

While my thoughts are in the clouds, Leo has moved closer to me and we are now standing inches apart, with my back toward his desk.

"I don't think friends stand this close to each other," I tease.

The heat radiating off his masculine body draws me closer to him.

"We can make up our own rules for what friends do." He puts his hand on my waist. "And I say that our friendship will involve me lifting you up on this desk and fucking you with my fingers."

His outspoken, raw honesty clouds the commonsense right out of my brain.

Grabbing my legs, Leo lifts me up and carries me to his desk.

His mouth plants deep, sensual kisses on mine.

Forget his fingers, I want to give him something he'll remember every time he's in this office.

I push him back with a force, cutting off our kiss. His eyes look ravenous and hungry for more.

Grabbing his tie, I push him down into his office chair.

"Mr. Forte." I stroke my palm over the massive bulge in his pants and reach for his zipper. "I'm so sorry I messed up that project you wanted me to do. I guess I'll have to make up for it somehow." Batting my eyelashes, I drop down to my knees in between his legs.

Leo smirks but does not fight me as I pull his pants and briefs down to the floor. His erection springs free. This man is definitely hung, and I'm hungry for every inch.

Taking my time, I plant sloppy wet kisses along his shaft.

Leo's hands find their way to my ponytail. He pulls the hair tie out and lets my hair fall free around my shoulders, and then he grabs a handful.

I move my tongue up his thick shaft and circle it around his tip. Hearing him moan encourages me to keep going. I slowly lick up and down his cock like a popsicle as he holds onto my hair.

When I've got him as far back into my mouth as possible, I moan. Letting the vibrations created in my mouth drive him absolutely wild. I go crazy with my tongue and then gently grab his balls and massage them in my hands.

"Stop." Leo reaches for my hands and face but I refuse to move. "I'm going to come." Staring up at him through tear streaked eyelashes, with my mouth full of his length, he shakes his head. "You're a crazy woman."

Pumping his shaft with my wet hands, he growls out my name before finishing in my mouth. I swallow and then lick my lips. Crawling up to him, I plant a kiss on his cheek.

"It was my pleasure," I whisper in his ear.

He looks at me like he wants to say something but just then a woman's loud voice fills the room through his intercom.

"*Signor Forte*, the conference is starting in five minutes."

"*Grazie*, Natalia, I'll be right out."

Moving away from Leo, I jump up off the ground in a panic. "I never set up those pastries." I grab the boxes. "We need to get to that conference room."

I can't believe I let him interfere with my job. I have never let a man come before work. This is new for me, same with giving a blowjob in an office.

Leo laughs with his pants still down around his ankles. "Don't worry, I don't think you'll get a bad report back to your boss. In fact, you'll get five stars for your service today."

After pulling up his pants, he moves behind me and swats my ass before we walk out of his office together. We stroll into the conference room and it's empty. I'm so thankful Italians are always late.

I quickly unload Marco's stunning works of art—cannoli, individual pieces of tiramisu, chocolate biscotti, and pizzelle cookies. After I finish displaying the treats, thankful that Marco sent me with plates and napkins, I try to find Leo to say goodbye.

Just then a rush of high-powered Italians glued to their cellphones stampede into the room like a herd.

Several people walk up to Leo and chat his ear off. I take this as my cue to secretly disappear. I can talk to my new 'friend' later. As I'm about to leave someone taps me on my shoulder.

"Excuse me. Don't I know you from somewhere?"

Oh no! I turn back around to see a brown haired, clean cut looking businessman who I guess is about 35. He's average height and has striking blue eyes. I would remember someone with eyes this blue.

"I'm sorry. I don't think so, maybe I have a twin out there some-where." I laugh off this stranger.

Leo has returned to my side and now both he and the stranger are staring at me, searching my face.

"Elena, this is Giorgio Piccolo. He's in charge of Research Marketing here at Forte Enterprises. And Giorgio, this is Elena Scott, she works at Stella's Caffé and delivered the amazing pastries over there."

Leo makes the introductions but Giorgio keeps his eyes glued to mine. I think he does know who I am and I'm suddenly freaking out.

"I've seen your face in a business magazine. No?"

"I can't say I know what you're talking about." I scoot closer to the door, trying not to get caught up in any more lies. The only person who knows about my business past is Marco, and that's the way I want to keep it. In Italy, I want to be your regular girl next door. And right now I want to run out of here as fast as I can.

"Maybe I am mistaken." Giorgio shrugs. "I'm sorry. It was nice to meet you, Elena." Giorgio and I shake hands and I turn back to Leo. He hasn't said anything since giving out the introductions.

I wonder if he is trying to place me from somewhere as well?

"Well, I should leave you to your meeting." I reach for the door handle as Leo puts his large hand on my lower back.

"It was nice seeing you, *bella*. I'm going to like this new friendship."

8

Leo calls me the next morning and invites me to the gym with him and then for a day to sightsee Italy as ... *friends*.

I want to see Italy and it doesn't hurt that an absolutely gorgeous guy wants to show me around his hometown. Exploring new places with locals guarantees you see the best spots.

You don't have to twist my arm.

We decide to meet at his normal, fancy upscale gym. We take a spin class together and then hit the punching bags. I love that he's willing to workout with me. In the past, the boyfriends I've dated would hit the weight section and ignore me until their session was over. What's the point of being at the gym with someone if you aren't actually with them?

After our grueling workout, I hit the locker room and jump in the shower, giddy with excitement for our day together. Did I really just say *giddy*? That's how giddy I am, I'm using words like giddy. Ugh, gag me.

After taking the quickest shower of my life and throwing on a pair of skinny denim jeans, black and white Converse sneakers, and a base-ball tee I leave the room in search of my man.

I mean, my *friend*.

Leo stands at the front of the door holding his gym bag and talking to a woman who looks overly excited. She has short brown hair and hazel eyes. I can't divert my gaze away from her tight pink sports bra and pair of booty shorts on her ridiculously sun kissed body.

She speaks Italian a million miles per minute, so fast that I can't understand a word she's saying. Of course this would happen to me. I'd run out looking like a wet haired teenager while yet another super-model is throwing herself at Leo.

Is this going to be the story of my life if I were to try to have a real relationship with him? Probably. I guess it's a good thing he took relationship off the table.

My heart still is a little frazzled about that. He can see the look on my face of confusion mixed with disgust. He pulls me into a one-armed hug and kisses the top of my head.

The Italian Barbie doll gives me the death stare as she looks me up and down. First, secretary girl and now gym girl.

Leo says a quick goodbye and tells her it was nice to meet her, and then hand-in-hand we walk out the door.

She must be a fan. I decide not to ask further questions.

Mateo is waiting outside in his usual black jacket and black pants with his black sunglasses—this must be his daily uniform.

Mateo asks us to set our gym bags down so he can put them in the trunk, and then he opens the door for us, and we climb into the town car.

I pull out my phone to send a quick text to my mom. She always wants me to check-in and I glance up to see Leo staring me down.

"You are in the company of an Italian man. Who could you possibly be texting?" he asks me with the curious look and then scoots over to sit right next to me before putting his arm around my shoulders.

"My mom." I hold up the phone. "I text her every few days so she doesn't worry. She's one of those moms who made me text her whenever I showed up at my friend's house if I drove myself ... until I was at least 20." I laugh, feeling a little homesick now.

"And what about your father?"

"He's a great guy. I wouldn't say I'm a daddy's girl, because he treated me, my brother, and my sister all equal. He works hard every day and then comes home to work hard even more." I smile thinking about my family. "Both of my parents went out of their ways to make sure us kids had everything we needed and more, even if they had to sacrifice themselves."

He takes a minute to really listen to my answer. "Sounds like there's a lot of love in your family." He smiles.

"Thanks! I'd say there is." I find a photo of my family on my phone and pass it over to him. "What about your parents?"

I'm hesitant to ask about his family because I'm not sure how much he is willing to share. From personal experience, I know those in the public eye like to keep a low profile.

Yet I don't know anything personal about him besides what I read in the gossip magazines and hear from Marco. I've been reminding myself to do a Google search on him, but now it would be too invasive.

"My parents were always smiling and holding hands. You could tell they were in love when you saw them. They were the kind of people who could make you sick with public displays of affection."

"You said they 'were.' Did something happen?"

Leo hesitates for a moment. I almost tell him that he doesn't need to answer but he continues.

"My father died when I was 13. He was killed in a motorcycle accident when he was driving to work one morning."

"I'm so sorry." I squeeze his hand that's now in my lap. "I can't even imagine the kind of pain your family went through."

My heart would shatter into a million pieces if I were to lose my dad.

Leo peers out the window. "After that, my mother became extremely depressed. To this day she still wears black almost all of the time. She isn't depressed anymore but she's a much rougher person around the edges now. And she became very protective of me after his death."

Leonardo seems too strong to need any protection, but the sentiment is sweet.

"Did she ever remarry?"

"No." He brings his attention back to me inside the car. "Outside of her work and her charity, I've never seen her talk to another man.

My father was her everything and she's never been the same without him."

"Do you have any brothers or sisters?" I ask.

"No, it's just me."

"Oh, too bad," I say, joking around with him.

"Why do you say that?"

"Well, you know what they say about people who are only children.

"What do they say?" he cocks his eyebrow.

"They say they're weirdos."

"*Weirdo?*" he says, in the most hilarious Italian accent, trying to mock me.

I bust out laughing and I can't stop! My stomach hurts and tears stream down my face. Oh great, there goes my mascara.

"Oh, you think that's funny?" Leo grabs my side and tickles me.

He did not just do that. I can't control myself when I'm being tickled. I go bat shit crazy. Screaming through exasperated breathes, my fight-or-flight reflexes take over and I accidentally swing my arm and, before he can duck, I hit him square in the jaw.

We both stop and stare at each other instantly. I can't believe I just hit him.

"Oh, my God, I am so sorry!"

He stares for just a second longer and then he busts out laughing.

I'm mortified but his contagious laugh causes me to laugh. We go on like this for a few more minutes and then let out loud sighs as our laughing wears us out.

We both lay back wearily in our seats for a breather.

"I can't believe you hit me." Leo rubs his red and somewhat swollen jaw. "I could call the police, and they'd send you to jail for assault. You know, I'm a very powerful man."

"Oh yeah?" I poke him in the side. "Only an only child weirdo would call the police on a girl!"

"*Cara*, I'll show you a weirdo when I play cop myself and take out the handcuffs." There's a growl to his raspy tone.

Instantly, the air changes between us.

Suddenly, it's hot in here.

"Where would you handcuff me?" I say, egging him on.

53

He leans in and whispers in my ear. "I can think of many places." He places soft kisses from my neck to my earlobe.

"Talk is cheap, *lover* boy." I place my hand on top of his firm thigh and give it a squeeze. "When you have the handcuffs ready, then we'll play."

In an instant, Leo pulls me onto his lap. I'm now straddling him. With my gaze locked on his sinful mouth, I frantically consume him. We both have a demanding possession over each other, with sweeping strokes of our tongues. I purr into his mouth and then return to kissing him deeply and slowly.

Pressing my cleavage against his hard chest, my nipples poke through my baseball tee. He pinches one between his fingers. I suck on his bottom lip then claim him with my tongue, slipping it in and out of his mouth.

Slowly, I grind against his cock through his pants. Circling my hips in just the right way causes a delicious friction to rub my clit between our clothes.

Leo pulls my tee over my head and takes off my bra. He cups my swollen breasts and I lean back as he sucks one nipple into his mouth before blowing across them.

This foreplay can't last for much longer. I have never wanted a man like this before and he keeps making me wait.

"Leo, I need to have you," I moan as he sucks vigorously on my other nipple now. I'm glad he doesn't play favorites.

Leo is quick and suddenly I'm lying on my back and he's towering over me in the backseat. He pulls off my sneakers and jeans. I'm left in my silky g-string.

His emerald eyes drink me in and then he runs his hand from my breasts and down to my stomach, and he cups my mound over my panties. Pushing my hips up, I grind into his hand, repeating the circling motion from our straddle.

Slowly he spreads my knees apart. Ripping my underwear off, he then licks my pussy with his warm tongue. I arch back and he slips his tongue into my slit. Every cell in my body is aware of his mouth. He flicks his tongue quickly over my clit.

Every muscle tenses and I quiver beneath him in desire.

His fingers move deeper into my cervix. I suck in a harsh breath as my legs twitch uncontrollably.

Squeezing my eyelids shut, I let the ripples rock through my core.

After I orgasm, Leo climbs back up my body and whispers in my ear, "It was my pleasure."

I see two can play at this game! I laugh at him turning my own game around on me.

"Your turn," I say with a ravenous gaze on him.

"No," he stops me, "this was all about you."

No man has ever made it all about me and now Leo has done it *twice*.

I can't get over how something erotic can touch my heart so deeply. He helps me put my clothes back on and he pulls me into his chest. I nuzzle up into him, and as I listen to his heartbeat, I nod off.

Post-sex vibes lull me to sleep.

———

I don't know how long I've been asleep; passing out in his cars seems to be a pattern for me. When I open my eyes, I see we are pulling up in front of a coral colored villa with green shutters on the many windows; potted plants sit on each windowsill.

"Where are we?" I look up from my protected area within Leo's strong arms.

"We're at my villa in Montalcino. Do you like it?"

Montalcino? We must have been in the car for more than two hours "How many houses do you have?"

"A few, here and there," he chuckles.

Mateo opens our door and has our gym bags waiting next to the entrance. I scoot off Leo's lap, and we both slide out of the town car. I stretch my legs. How long was that ride? I see Leo talking to Mateo, giving him instructions. Outside the hustle and bustle of Roma, Leo looks so much calmer and even younger.

Leo opens the front door and waves me over. I go to grab my gym bag, and Mateo beats me to it. "I'll bring it in for you, *signora*. You'll

55

never have to carry your own bags if I'm around. That's my job and I'm happy to do it."

"You are too kind. *Grazie.*"

He nods.

I walk into the villa with Leo. The villa is open with large windows near the back of the house. Stunning paintings hang on the walls and bright colors are everywhere on art, on lamps, on tables, and on rugs that sit on top of marble floors.

"Let me give you the tour." Leo puts his hand on my elbow and leads me into an open kitchen with its white and black marble and stainless steel appliances.

This place makes my apartment, which I thought was nice, look like a homeless shelter.

"Can you cook?" I ask him curiously.

All of the appliances look brand new and top of the line. But I, admittedly, have no clue what these can do. I do, however, notice an impressive espresso machine. Now *that* would make Marco jealous! I fight the urge to take a selfie with it and text it to him.

"No, I could handle the basics—toast and eggs. The appliances are for my chef."

Outside of the kitchen sits the living room. There's a fireplace surrounded by stone, a flatscreen TV on the wall, a black leather couch, and two chairs. There's a glass set of double doors.

Stepping outside, the sun shines over a huge crystal clear blue swimming pool. In the distance, I see the famous vineyards of Montalcino.

"Want to go for a swim?"

I turn around and see Leo giving me his signature stare, like he's drinking me in again.

"I don't have a bathing suit." I shrug.

"I asked Mateo to pick one up along the way, when you were enjoying a little nap."

I stare at him in shock. Is he serious? This is a man with a plan. "Okay, show me this bathing suit."

"Follow me," he says as he turns back into the villa. We walk up a set of stairs past the living room, and I see a row of doors. He leads me to the last door on the left and lets me know that this is my room and everything I need is already inside.

I walk into an orange painted bedroom with a queen size bed and a blue comforter. Sitting on the bed is a purple string bikini, the smallest bikini I've ever seen.

Was this a joke? I might as well swim naked.

I strip off my clothes and put on the teeny tiny purple bikini just so I can take it off and complain about it after. I notice that the bedroom has its own bathroom. I get a look at myself in the mirror and I have to admit, I look good. This bikini fits in all the right places and hugs my curves. I wasn't sure my giant ass was going to fit in it, but damn. I stare at myself for a moment, remembering what Leo and I did in the limo.

I smile thinking about his lips and tongue all over me. I love what we've been doing but I am dying to have sex with him.

Never in my life have I wanted a man inside of me more than I want Leo. What is he waiting for? If we don't have sex soon I'm going to die.

When did I become this needy?

With the dirty thoughts out of my mind, I grab the pink beach towel from the bed and walk back to the pool.

Leo isn't outside yet, so I spread my towel out on a lounge chair and I lay back to get my tan on. Closing my eyes, I allow myself to relax. A few minutes later, I hear the sliding door open and I open my eyes.

Leo towers over me, standing next to my lounge chair.

"That bathing suit suites you." Leo looks down at me like I'm the juiciest peach on the platter.

I'd compliment the way his tight blue board shorts fit him just right, but I know he's already aware. His chest is broad, his arms are strong, and he has a ridiculously toned six pack.

"Ready?" I stand now and turn to walk toward the pool.

"Si, *cara*. I'm ready, but are you?"

Before I know better, I'm flying into the pool.

After coming up from under the warm water I scream, "Oh, my God! I can't believe you threw me!"

"No, I did not. Prove it."

"Prove it?" I question back at him.

Are we in sixth grade right now? Before I can answer, he's doing a cannonball into the pool, landing right next to me.

"I'll prove it, all right." I splash water in his face.

He laughs, and the next thing I know, he's picking me up and throwing me to the far end of the pool. With all this water torture, he's lucky I know how to swim.

"You're a bully, Leonardo!" I say after regaining my composure.

He swims over and backs me against the edge of the pool. He is so close to me that the water droplets dripping from his dark eyelashes land on my cleavage.

Wrapping my arms around his neck and my legs around his waist, I pull myself as close to him as I can get.

"Sorry for being a bully." Leo leans in to suck on my lower lip.

I run my fingers through his wet hair, and he slips his tongue into my mouth. He circles his tongue around mine, and we kiss for what feels like hours. I love kissing Leo.

As he pushes against me, I feel his erection growing. Looks like he loves kissing me, too.

He takes one hand off the edge of the pool, unties the strings of my bikini top, and throws it out of the pool. His hand cups my wet breast, and he uses his thumb to circle over my nipple. I lean into him and suck the water droplets off his neck before I bite down on him.

"Trying to leave a mark?" Leo cocks an eyebrow at me.

"A love bite," I purr into his ear.

The next thing I know, he's untying the strings of my bikini bottoms and throwing those out of the pool as well.

Leo runs his hands up and down my thighs, stopping just before my pussy. I can't take much more. He runs his hands up my thighs one more time before one finger is inside of me.

Pushing my hand into his tight swim trucks, I grab his manhood with both hands. While I'm showing his erection some love with my hands, his thumb circles my clit applying gentle pressure, and I'm in heaven. This man's hands are magical. I lean my head back and moan, and then two fingers are inside of me. He fucks me with his fingers, and I'm on the edge of exploding.

"I need you." I moan out in between moments of pure ecstasy. "I want you inside of me. Please." I can't believe I'm begging him. I'm usually the girl who has sex with her boyfriends just so they'll shut up about it, not for pleasure.

"Come for me, Elena," he commands with a raspy growl. And, as if on cue, I orgasm. To hold back from screaming, I sink my teeth into his wet shoulder.

When I briefly regain composure, no longer seeing stars, I grip his cock and pump him faster. Seconds later, I feel his massive cock throb and this time it's him moaning into my neck.

"Dios mio. I can't believe you just commanded that orgasm out of me." I limply hang on to his body while we float around the pool.

He laughs. "You never had anyone to do that before."

"Definitely can't say I have. Let's just say my previous boyfriends didn't command anything out of me, because I usually faked it," I say, laughing. I can't believe I just told him that.

He grabs my chin and pushes it up to look at him.

"Cara, you have not been with the right men."

The summer Italian sun beats down on us as he looks into my eyes. "At this moment, I'd have to agree with you. And I'd also like to add you are going to need to clean this pool."

I laugh and lean in to kiss him again. We swim over to the edge of the pool, and he jumps out and looks back down at me.

"Well, aren't you coming?"

"Commanding me to come again? I don't think this time it will work." I laugh, floating around in the pool. "I'm naked, don't you remember?"

"Oh, I remember. Now get out so we can go get some dinner."

"I'm not getting out. What if someone sees me?"

"You are worried about someone seeing you now." He smirks. "What about a few minutes ago? You didn't seem to mind if a stranger or the help saw all of that."

I wasn't even thinking! My cheeks heat up.

Is anyone else at Leo's house? Where's Mateo? I keep letting Leo do what he wants with me in public places.

He's still staring at me, and I can see it in his eyes that he doesn't think I'll have the nerve to get out of the pool. As he starts to walk over to grab my towel, I decide to give him a show. #ScrewIt

I strut out of the pool, birthday suit and all.

"You are absolutely breathtaking," he says, as he looks me up and down, handing me my towel.

"Stop drooling, lover boy, and get that dinner going."

Leo gives me some time to settle into my bedroom before dinner. I hope this is going to be a late night. If not, I'm going to ditch this guy forever because I don't think I can face him if he doesn't want to be intimate, all the way intimate with me.

With my late night in mind, I shoot a quick text to Marco letting him know I won't be coming in tomorrow. I think he'd excuse me for taking his advice by getting to know Leo.

I jump into the shower to get the chlorine smell off me. I let my natural curls air dry and skip the makeup. I put on a pair of black leggings, a red strapless bra with some cute red lace panties, and an off the shoulder long sleeve purple sweatshirt. It's not glamorous, but it will do for lounging around the villa.

The smells from the kitchen draw me closer. Seduction by food. I turn the corner into the kitchen and see the lights are dim and candles stand everywhere leading into the dining room.

On the table sits a bouquet of long-stemmed red roses. Some champagne chills on ice, and the table is set with fine china. But the room is empty.

Where the heck is my Italian lover?

Oh great, now's he got me using the term 'lover' as well. #Embarrassing

Taking a whiff of the divine roses, I can't help but smile that they are my favorite. I don't like many flowers, but these are my favorite. Before I can pull out my chair, a large hand cups my ass.

Leo spins me around and plants a kiss on my lips and then on my exposed shoulder.

"Do you like roses, *bella*?" He pulls me into his chest.

"Mi amo roses. These are lovely, as well as all the candles. Did you go to all this trouble?"

"It wasn't trouble at all. Just wait until you see what's for dinner."

"Did you cook?" I give him a skeptical look.

How long was I in the shower?

"I'd love to take the credit for all of this, but credit goes where it's due. Mateo set up the candles and roses, while Gemma made dinner."

"Gemma?" There's another woman here?

"Si, the lady who makes everything run smoothly in my life."

"Are you trying to make me jealous?"

"Is it working?"

"A little," I laugh at this super immature conversation.

"Gemma is my housekeeper and chef ... she's also in her fifties and is married with two children."

"Did you add that last part to let me know that she's not a threat?"

"Did it help?"

I give him a little shove and take my seat at the table.

Leo grabs the champagne and pops the cork, pouring us each a glass in crystal flutes. He hands me mine, and we toast to getting to know each other better. Before I can even put my glass down, a salad plate is in front of me. I turn to look back at whom so quickly put the plate under my nose, but no one is in the room.

I dig into my Caprese salad and realize I haven't eaten since breakfast. This guy better watch out because nothing comes between this girl and her food. I finish my salad, and the most delicious plate of cheese ravioli with marinara sauce is placed in front of me. This time I catch a quick glimpse of the back of the mysterious Gemma, but she's out of the dining room before I can even say a quick *"Grazie."*

The cheese ravioli is to die for. It's hands down the best meal I've had since coming to Italy. As I'm devouring my food, I notice that Leo has stopped eating and is looking at me.

"See something you like?" I say mockingly to him, putting my fork down and wiping my mouth with my napkin.

"Si, you."

"Me? What could you possibly be staring at when you have the most delicious meal in front of you? Eat up, man."

"Don't worry about me, I will eat. I just enjoy watching you eat. It's cute."

"Cute? What do you mean *cute?*"

"You make these little moans when you take a bite you love. You appreciate your meals." He smiles at me. "It's not often a woman can let herself enjoy her food."

"Clearly, you've never been on a date with a fat girl who likes to eat." I tease.

And if they do like to eat, I'd bet they puke up their meals after.

"Don't call yourself fat in front of me ever again," he says, turning serious. "You are far from it, and I will not let you put yourself down like that." He says this with such a command that I feel like I'm in trouble.

"Sir, yes, sir. I had no idea you were such a drill sergeant."

"This is not a joke, Elena. You have an amazing body. You have sexy curves, delicious breasts and an ass that I want to bite or spank every time I see it."

This man is something else. First he seduces me, then he feeds me, then he scolds me, and now he is giving me a big ego.

"*Grazie.* You aren't bad, either, I guess." I wink and run my fingers up his bicep and give it a little squeeze.

"You are trouble, *bella.* Finish your ravioli. Or else."

I poke a ravioli with my fork. "Again with the commands. Are you always this bossy?"

"Yes."

We sit in silence and finish our meals. I can't believe how at ease I am with him. The moments of silence feel comfortable, not like the usual getting to know someone awkwardness.

After the dinner made in heaven, Leo and I settle into the living room. There's a fire going and the lights are now dim here too. We sit down in front of a lush bearskin rug and sip more champagne.

Slow down, girl, you do not want a drunken repeat of the other day's ridiculous hangover.

Leo puts down his glass and scoops my bare feet into his lap. He rubs them with just the right amount of pressure. "So tell me, what brought you to Italy?"

I sit for a second and watch him rub my feet. "I was just bored and ready for a change."

"So when you get bored of Italy, will you need a change again?"

Where is he going with this? Is he worried about me leaving him? That can't be; he's made it clear that he doesn't want a long term thing. Maybe that's why he wants me? Because he thinks I'll be leaving?

I have no clue what the future holds.

"What did your family say when you left?"

"At first they didn't understand why I wanted to go so far away from home. But they knew I was getting burnt out from day-to-day life." I shrug. "I wasn't really happy where I was. In the end they gave me their blessing."

Leo switches to rub the other foot. "I'm glad to hear that. Their blessing led to *this ... us*," he says.

"That was super cheesy, but I loved hearing you say that."

Before he can ask me more questions about the life I'm trying to keep secret, I decide to turn the tables back to him

"So, tell me more about you. How did you end up employing Mateo and Gemma? They seem very devoted to you."

"They are like *a mia famiglia*. I am equally devoted to helping them whenever they need me. Both Gemma and Mateo worked for my parents. I've can't remember a time when they weren't in my life."

"Wow. Did they always have the roles they have now?"

"Mateo worked security for my father's company, and then when my father passed away Mateo became my personal driver and body-guard. He took me to school and soccer practice, and he did every-thing a parent would do because my mom was so distant. She was holed up in her room depressed."

I didn't expect to hear that they were so close. No wonder Mateo was trying to get me to see the good in Leo. He's known him since he was a boy. He's much more than just a driver.

"What about Gemma? Was she always a chef?"

"No, Gemma was my nanny and later turned into our chef and housekeeper. We had a bigger staff growing up, but my mom let a lot of those people go when my father died."

"And your mom just let you take her staff?"

"*Si,* I can be persuasive." Leo winks at me. "My mom knew Gemma and Mateo were my friends, sometimes the only people I had in my life, more than just 'the help.'"

Thinking of Leo as a little boy, without a father and with a depressed mother, holed up in a big mansion all alone, breaks my heart. I find myself feeling a strange devotion to these kind people who take care of him too.

While this serious conversation took place, Leo never once stopped rubbing my feet.

When I think he's going to move up my leg, he bites down on the sole of my foot. Completely catching me off guard, I spill the champagne out of my glass on the hardwood floor.

"Oh, my God! I can't believe you just bit me." I stand up.

"Where are you going?" He stares at me with laser focused eyes.

"To the kitchen. I need to get some paper towels and clean this mess up ... duh."

He pulls me down, and now I'm lying on top of him. We are face to face, and I'm suddenly breathing heavy. This whole experience has my heart racing.

"I guess I won't be going to the kitchen."

"Quiet, *bella*, you don't always have to say something sarcastic."

He instantly rolls us around and now he is on top of me. Grinding up against him, he snickers. Leo grinds back against me; creating an intense friction between us.

He takes his attention to my neck which he both kisses and nibbles on. I wrap my legs around his body.

Leo pulls us up, and now I'm sitting in his lap with my legs still wrapped around him. My hands are in his thick hair, and then he lifts them over my head to take off my sweatshirt and unclasp my bra. He rubs my breasts, and I lean back so he can get a better view. He smiles and lowers his head to my chest to suck on my nipples.

The things Leo can do with his tongue.

Deciding I want to be in charge, I lift off his shirt and run my nails down his chest through his dark brown hair. Normally, chest hair turns me off, but Leo has just the right amount to turn me on. Not too hairy, but not bare like a boy.

64

Leo lays me back and slips my leggings slowly down my legs, and then my panties. I'm lying naked against the luxurious bearskin rug. Combine that with the heat coming from the fire *and* my body, and it's a deadly combination.

Leo strips from his dark blue jeans and boxer briefs. I admire his chiseled body. He kneels down on the rug and spread my knees apart. I smell the scent of my desire, and he hasn't even touched there yet.

Before I can beg, he dips his head to my sex and runs his tongue in circles around my clit. I thrust my hips up and grind into his mouth.

I want him inside me ... now. For our first time.

"Don't make me beg any longer," I plead.

The next minute he is reaching for a condom. He props himself up on each side of me on his elbows. We lock eyes, and the head of his cock touches my wet entrance. He rubs in back and forth without actually slipping himself inside of my sex.

"You're killing me!" I moan and try grinding my sex against him.

"Bella, I'm in charge. I'll make you wait." He smiles down at me.

Over my dead body!

He kisses me deeply and slowly. It's so sensual I almost forget about this tempting cock, that is until he pushes inside of me. I am so wet; he slides right in but he's bigger than I'm used to. It takes a second for me to adjust to the pressure. When he groans and pushes deeper inside me, every sense heightens within.

"You are so tight." Leo pulls out of me.

He slips himself back inside as the thrusts of his hips grow harder and faster. When I don't think I'll be able to last much longer, I claw my nails into his back as I hold on while he pulses.

We are both sweaty from the fire burning next to us and our bodies are slick against one another.

Anticipation buildes deep inside me. His teeth meet my lower lip, and he pulls on it. Pushing me over the edge, the climax takes control as we both quiver and orgasm together.

He collapses on top of me, and I wrap my arms around him, holding him to my chest as close as I possibly can. It's silent except for our heavy breathing while we both try to calm down. At some point he pulls out of me. We fall asleep in each other's arms in front of a dying fire. #ItWasWorthTheWait

———

This time I know where I am when I wake up in Leo's bedroom. And this time he's in the bed with me. I take advantage of the fact that he's sound asleep as I study his handsome face. He looks relaxed and boyish while sleeping.

Lifting the covers, I peek under to notice we are both still very naked. Deciding to repay him for always being a generous lover to me, I crawl beneath the blankets, finding his hard length waiting for me. Sliding both my hands up his shaft, I hear Leo moan.

"Good morning, Elena." He pulls the sheets down to grab a fistful of my hair.

I let out a small chuckle and then lick him like a lollipop. He tenses, and I run my lips gently up and down his penis until I get to the tip. I swirl my tongue around it and then suck it with a little more force. He lets out a little growl, and then I take him deep into the back of my throat.

I run my hands up his thighs while my mouth drives him crazy. He hisses above me between his clenched teeth and orgasms into my mouth while panting my name. I swallow what he's left behind and then crawl back up the bed to give him a kiss.

"I can get used to waking up like that every morning," he grins. We are lying facing each other; he's propped up on his elbow. He reaches over to skim his fingers against my hard nipples. "I see you like it, too." He gives my nipple a squeeze.

"I love giving you pleasure. It turns me on, too."

He rolls on top of me and flicks his tongue into my mouth. I shove him off me and jump out of the bed in search of my clothes.

"Settle down, lover boy. Enough sex ... for now."

"Enough sex?" He laughs. "You were just begging me for it."

"I have something in mind for us to do." I pull my leggings back on.

"Oh, yeah? And what is that?"

"Go get your sneakers. We are going for a run."

I leave Leo to throw on some running clothes while I go to my bedroom to grab my sneakers. I'm downstairs before Leo and the strong scent of espresso leads me to the kitchen.

Standing at the island putting egg frittatas on two plates is an older red haired woman. She looks up to meet my gaze.

"You must be the infamous Gemma."

"Guilty! Nice to meet you, the also infamous Elena." She points to the kitchen table before grabbing the plates and heading there herself.

She sits both plates down and then walks back to get the coffees.

"Thank you so much. This looks delicious."

"Grazie," she thanks me and, when she's not looking, I take a hard look at her. She's a shorter, stockier woman probably five foot at the most. She has shoulder length fiery red hair and looks like a great Italian mom with a 'caring but won't take shit from anyone' air about her.

Leo walks into the room looking just as incredible in his black track jacket and pants as he does in suits and jeans. He leans over to give me a quick kiss on the cheek before taking his seat beside me.

"Buon giorno, Gemma." Leo greets her as she brings over our espressos.

"Buon giorno, signor Forte. Can I get you two anything else?"

"No, breakfast looks great. *Grazie "*

Leo and I eat and chat easily over our frittatas and espressos, and then we head outside to start our run.

The sun beats down on us but the air is crisp this early in the morning which makes it the ideal running weather. As we pick up the pace, I admire the prettiest hill town I've ever seen. You'll never find views like this in the Motor City.

"Come on, Mr. Beautiful, show me what you got." I take off in a sprint.

He follows after me and quickly catches up.

I slow down a bit and we settle into a jog side by side. It's nice to have someone with me during a run; I am usually always alone. I didn't realize that until right now. We don't have to talk, just keep our strides, take in the scenery of the hills, and listen to our breathing in sync.

There's a picturesque old fortress, olive trees, grapevines, and country-side to see.

After running for what feels like miles, I spot a small park ahead and ask him to take a break. This looks like a nice spot to stretch and relax for a few minutes before starting the long run back to the villa. I find a park bench, do a couple stretches, and then join Leo sitting on the grass.

Across the park there's a mom and her two kids—a little boy pushing a little girl on the swing set. They are laughing. I catch myself staring at them while Leo is staring at me.

"Do you like kids?" I ask, not to pressure him, more out of curiosity.

"Of course."

"That's not an 'of course' type of answer. Some people don't like kids."

"Do you like kids, Elena?"

"Of course ... duh!"

"Always with the sarcasm." He tackles me to the ground and tickles me.

I bust out laughing. "Enough! Enough! We are going to scare the kids! You remember what happened last time you tickled me. Do you want to get punched again?" I shout between squeals and notice the tables have turned; the family is now staring at us.

We lay back in the grass to look up at the sky, and Leo reaches for my hand.

"Have you ever been in love?" I hear myself ask before I realize it was probably too soon. Why couldn't I just keep my thoughts to myself?

"No. I don't believe in love."

"Did I hear you wrong? You don't *believe* in love? I didn't know it was something that you had the choice to believe in or not."

"Why wouldn't it be?"

"Because it's love." I sit up to stare down at him. "Love is every-where. Parents love their children, and children love their parents. Husbands love their wives, wives love their husbands."

"Well, that's where I'd have to stop you. I don't believe in marriage, either."

"No marriage for you ... or others?"

"I don't really care what others do, Elena. No marriage for me."

Laying back down, I keep my eyes on the sky and take in what he just revealed. This must be what he meant by no long term anything when we talked in his office.

Don't get me wrong, I'm not ready to wear a white dress anytime soon, but I did make that stupid wish in the Trevi Fountain.

And now I'm spending all my time with someone who doesn't wish for the same.

Not now, or ever.

————

We run back to the villa in silence. When we walk through the door, Gemma tells us lunch is ready and she'll serve us outside by the pool. We sit down at a patio table, and some fresh lemonade and panini.

"Is something wrong?" Leo asks.

I am not about to talk about marriage or a future with Leo again after he told me he doesn't want it. I knew that yet I still agreed to come here.

Already knowing that, how can I still be so upset?

This is my fault. But it doesn't make it any easier on my heart, which is growing a strong attachment to him.

"Nope." I shove a piece of sandwich into my mouth.

"A one word answer from the woman who always has a lot to say. I would say that *does* mean something is wrong." Leo places his sandwich down on his plate.

"Not a thing." Another bite goes into my mouth. "I do think that it's time to head home, though. I have to be at work tomorrow to open."

Back to reality and enough of this make believe.

"Back in America, what did you do for work?"

"I dabbled in a few things here and there." I pick up my now empty plate and bring it back into the house. Leo follows behind me.

"If you don't want to share your past with me, Elena, that's okay."

"It's not that I don't want to share, it's just that it's not that exciting compared to yours." Even though Gemma is here, I hand wash our plates and leave them out to dry.

"Okay, *bella*, I believe you. And I'll tell Mateo to bring the car around, but just so you know, you can always stay as long as you like."

Even though he believes that to be true, I know our time together has an expiration date.

9

"You are starting to get the hang of things," Marco says.

It's early on a Wednesday morning and Marco is teaching me how to make panettone before we open. Once the customers flock in, there is no extra time to teach me how to bake.

The day carries on with our usual pace and it's not until my body goes on alert that I know he's in the building.

"Ciao Signor Forte! Mi chiamo Marco. It's a pleasure to meet you. We are honored that you enjoy Stella's." Marco rushes up to Leo like he's a celebrity. Well, I guess he's kind of a celebrity here.

"Thank you! It's nice to meet you. I've heard great things about you from Elena." Leo shakes Marco's hand.

I can't get over Leo's sexy look today: stubble on his face, a black leather jacket, a tight gray t-shirt, dark jeans, and a pair of Converse. He definitely doesn't look like he's heading to the office.

He catches me looking at him like he's a piece of meat. Italian sausage, perhaps.

"Where are you headed ... or is this the new look for the office?"

"I don't have to go into the office today." Leo leans into the counter. "I have a phone conference at one, but a suit isn't required for that. I was hoping you could skip out on work to join me. I brought my motorcycle."

Picturing myself on the back of his bike with my thighs pressed against this back and my arms wrapped around his chiseled chest turns me on.

Who knew he'd be my real life Italian version of Jax Teller?

"Earth to Elena." Leo waves his hand in front of my face. "Where do you go when you space out like that?"

"Space out? I was just deep in thought."

"Well, Spacey, I really wanted to spend time with you today because I have to go out of town until Saturday for work."

He hasn't left the building yet and I already miss him. Wow, I don't think I have gone that long without him since we've met.

"Are you telling me this because you are going to be so desperately lonely without me?"

"No, because I know *you* will be desperately lonely without me."

"Look at you with the smart answers now. The tables have turned." I notice the place is starting to fill up again.

Leo notices a line begin to form too. "Well, I don't want to hold you back from work, but I do want to give you this." He hands me a thick red envelope and then leans over the counter to kiss me quickly. I slip the envelope into my back pocket.

As he's leaving, it's just my luck *Signora* Lucca watched the whole thing.

"Elena!" Her jaw drops. "You didn't tell me you knew Signor Forte!" She waves her hand in front of her face as if she's hot. "Listen, even though he's a *bello* billionaire, don't give up on my doctor. I'm telling you, call him."

Starting to make her usual drink, I say, "*Grazie* for your advice, *Signora* Lucca."

After a steady stream of customers, I find a moment to myself and take out the red envelope that's been burning a hole in my pocket. The black invitation reads:

You're Exclusively Invited!
Leonardo Forte's Birthday Bash

Saturday, 10pm
Club Luciano

He came to invite me to his birthday party. Who knew a man like Leo would even have a birthday party. I haven't been there yet but I know Club Luciano is a posh, upscale club.

What will I wear?

And will supermodels be there too?

———

Strutting into the club after blowing a ton of money on a shopping spree, I feel like a million bucks. The tight red floor length dress has a long slit up the side revealing way too much leg but the sales woman convinced me I had to have it.

The sweetheart cut gave me room to display a large black crystal necklace right above my cleavage, which I'm also showing off.

Eat your heart out, Birthday Boy!

With my VIP invitation, I skip the long line of people standing outside the club. I don't recognize anyone I know inside so I head straight to the bar. I find a spot to weasel my way up, and a handsome bartender greets me.

He has on a tight black t-shirt and jeans that show off his muscular arms, which are lined with tattoos.

His crystal blue eyes scan my face. "*Ciao, bella.* What can I get for you?"

"Prosecco."

He hands me back the drink, and I take out some cash.

"It's on the house." He winks.

"*Grazie.*"

Minding my own business and sipping my drink, a warm hand lands on my lower back. I quickly turn around, ready to fight off the bar creep, when I look into Leo's warm green eyes.

Just like the other day at the coffee shop, he's still rocking the stubble. I can't wait for that to rub against my thighs.

"Well, hello, birthday boy." I lean in for a kiss.

73

He puts my drink on the bar, pulls me into him, and deepens the kiss. Why do I feel like he's staking his claim in front of the bartender and anyone else watching?

His large hands roam over my dress, and he cups my ass and presses me into his firm body. Against my belly, he pushes his hard bulge.

Would it be wrong to skip his own birthday party?

"Aren't you going to introduce us to your little friend?" says a woman with a thick, high pitched Italian accent.

Pulling away from Leo's kiss, I see a tall brunette with long ombre hair next to me. She's wearing a cute black mini dress with everything on display—from her long olive legs to her full cleavage.

"I'm Victoria." She extends her hand to me.

"Elena, nice to meet you," I say, shaking her hand back.

"Come on, Elena, let me bring you to the VIP area to meet the rest of my friends."

Leo cuts off Victoria's introduction and escorts me toward the back of the club past a roped off area.

I spot an Italian A list couple that I saw on this week's cover of TMZ Italia—the article must have been wrong because they look very much together. There are also two politicians standing around a tall table in what looks like a heated debate, their wives looking bored behind them. Beside them, I spot singers, actors, and A listers; it's like I stepped into a glamorous wonderland.

"Leonardo!"

A short man dressed in an impeccable Gucci suit comes rushing up to us and embraces Leo with a hug and traditional European double cheek kiss.

"Arturo, I'd like to introduce you to Elena." Leo pulls me closer into his side. It doesn't slip past me that he doesn't include a title when he introduces me—definitely not *girlfriend.*

"It's nice to meet you, Arturo," I try to spit out as Arturo pulls me from Leo and plants the same double cheek kiss on me.

He seems nice enough, but his soggy kisses and grabby hands send off a gross vibe.

"Elena, it's nice to meet you, b*ella.*" Arturo gives me a look up and down.

Leo notices a shift in my stance and holds my hand, giving it a little squeeze of assurance.

"Glad you could make it, Arturo." Leo pulls me along to work the room.

We say *'ciao'* to plenty of nice people, and after making the rounds, he and I settle into a back booth by ourselves.

"What are you thinking?" Leo asks.

"Your friends are nice ... and very glamorous."

"No one as glamorous as you. You look absolutely stunning tonight." He scoots closer so our legs are right up against one another.

Leo pushes my hair off my shoulder and leans in to kiss my neck. Yes, I can confirm, his stubble against my skin turns me on.

"You and public places. You are always trying to get me into trouble, Birthday Boy." I trail my hand up his thigh.

His eyes giving me a smoldering look.

"*You* are the trouble here," he whispers into my ear as his hand lands on the slit of my dress and slowly trails up my leg.

He runs his fingers up and down my thigh, just barely missing my sex. With his other hand, he grabs my chin and pulls me into a passionate kiss. His tongue thrusts into my mouth and swirls around my own.

"Leo," I moan.

His large hands push my thighs apart. I grab his blazer and pull him in closer.

Before I can let him peel my black lace panties down, he takes matters into his own hands and rips them off.

Leo massages my clit with my own juices, and then he slips a finger inside of me. My sex is throbbing. I want to scream out, but I bite it back, remembering where we are.

He slips another finger inside and then sucks on my earlobe. I can't hold back, I shut my eyes and surrender to what he's doing to me. Thrusting his fingers in and out, I let go. After I finish convulsing, he takes his fingers out of my sex and, without breaking my gaze, he sucks on them.

Oh my gosh.

"How do you always do this to me?" I lean in to give his cheek a kiss.

"Your juices are so sweet. And you, my dear, are so lovely."

My skin feels flushed and damp. I can't believe I've let him take me in public ... *again.*

"Okay you sex maniac, I need to excuse myself to go freshen up in the bathroom."

Leo laughs and smacks my ass as I slide out of the booth.

I don't forget that I am now without panties, where did he put those? Thank God there was a tablecloth covering us, or Italy's rich and famous would have gotten quite the R rated show.

———

In the bathroom I take a second to give myself a hard look in the mirror. *What am I doing?* Letting a hot billionaire finger me at his birthday party in a crowded club full of influential people.

This is not what I'm used to. I mean, it feels amazing, but this is so far out of my comfort zone. If I don't pull it together, I am going to get more attached than I already am and it's going to hurt like hell when we have to split up.

But what if we don't have to split up?

Am I crazy?

Why did I just think that?

Of course we have to break up.

He doesn't believe in love, marriage, or being anything other than 'lovers.' I still don't quite know what that means for us.

But do I need marriage?

Maybe I can settle for being on his arm for as long as he'll have me.

I remind myself that after tonight's party we need to talk again.

Leaving the bathroom, I walk toward he VIP area when I spot Victoria and Arturo standing at the bar talking rather loudly. I turn to head over to where I left Leo when I hear Victoria's high pitched voice ring out.

"I can't believe he brought that broke ass, trashy American to his birthday party."

"And to think this guy could have any woman he wants. What a waste!" Arturo adds, looking just as stuck up and annoyed as Victoria.

What the fuck? They turn around to walk back to the roped off area, and I quickly duck back into bathroom before they can spot me.

What a bunch of shit talkers.

Trying to hold back my emotions seems impossible but this is Leo's birthday party and I will not let anything ruin this day for him ... even his pair of crappy friends.

When I decide it's safe to leave the bathroom after I regain my composure, I walk behind the ropes of the VIP area and notice that there are plenty more people in the room since I stepped out.

Couples dance, drinks flow, and everyone is having a great time. But where is the Birthday Boy? He's not in the booth.

Spotted!

He's standing in the corner of the room with his back to me. My eyes would be drawn to that sexy ass anywhere. I walk toward him when he steps to the side and I notice he's not alone.

He's standing with none other than supermodel Aurora Rossi.

And he's not just standing with her ... they are kissing! Her hands are on his biceps, holding herself close to him. His hands are on her waist.

The entire room seems to go into black tunnel vision, and I swear I am going to faint.

I have to leave before he sees me! They pull apart and turn around, but I duck behind the bar inside the VIP room.

"*Scusi*, are you okay?" Hot bartender man catches me crouched down behind his bar looking like a damn fool on the verge of tears.

I refuse to let my confusion and heartbreak show.

"Oh, you know, just playing a game of hide and seek." I peek over the bar to make sure the coast is clear.

He crouches down next to me, and I can smell his Dolce and Gabbana Light Blue cologne.

"Who are we hiding from?" he says up close to my face with a little smirk.

"Just some jerk." I peer around the bar. "He's out of sight now. Thanks for letting me hide out behind here. It was nice to meet you."

Running out of the club, I can't hear his reply and he can't see the tears slide down my trashy American face.

50 missed calls.

25 missed text messages.

Leo has blown up my phone after I ran out of the club and came home to eat my weight worth of gelato. The man in the ice cream shop must have spotted the heartbreak in my eyes and gave me the food for free.

Pity gelato is still gelato.

Rolling over in my warm bed, I wish I was the kind of person who was good at sleeping in. I'd prefer to spend this Sunday morning hiding from the rest of the world.

There's no point in wasting the day away because I've cried out all my tears. I make my way to the kitchen which is conveniently just a few feet away from the bedroom.

After making a protein shake, I prop open my laptop and write a quick email to my Sophie. Before I can hit 'send,' my phone rings, and Sophie's name pops up on my screen for a FaceTime call.

Great minds think alike.

"Hey Sophie!" Her face pops up on my screen. "What's going on, girl?"

"Elena!" She waves a small Italian flag in front of the screen. "How the hell have you been, you sexy bitch? I haven't gotten a chance to talk to you in weeks."

Oh, how I missed this girl. Sophie is the toughest chick I know. We met in the seventh grade when we had a bunch of classes together. We weren't the typical girls who had superficial "BFF" bracelets—true friends thick and thin, without needing to display it to the world.

"I've missed your sassiness so much. Things are going good over here in beautiful *Italia*. How's life back in the mitten?"

"Same ol' shit. Now, for real, spill the beans! What the heck have you been doing? You find yourself a hunky Italian stud to shack up with yet?" She raises her perfectly arched eyebrows.

"Do people really say *shack up*?" I laugh. "How old are you?"

"You know what I mean. Answer the question."

"Yes, there's a stud, but that's over now."

"Over?" She pulls her phone screen closer to her face. "What for? Did you have a one night stand?" Sophie brings her manicured hand up to her mouth in fake shock. "Whoa! Italy has changed you, my good little friend."

Pointing my index finger at her, I say, "Slow your roll, Sophie. You are out of your mind."

My best friend is officially *pazza*.

"Stop dancing around the topic here. Tell me about this mystery man."

"His name is Leonardo Forte, and it was a quick fling that ended last night after he pretty much made a clown of me at a club."

She rapidly flutters her eyelashes. "Wait. *The* Leonardo Forte ... the billionaire?"

"Hold on a second ... how the do *you* know about him?"

"We learned about him in my marketing class. I even wrote a section about him in my senior business proposal." Sophie picks up an iced coffee and takes a sip. "What the heck is going on with the sexy billionaire? Tell me before I fall over."

"Okay, okay, don't get your panties in a bunch. Here goes ..."

I launch into the whole story, sparing the TMI sex details, and end with the humiliating scene in the club where Leo cheated on me with a supermodel in front of everyone.

Does it count as cheating if we were just 'friends with benefits'? I'm so torn about what I'm allowed to feel right now.

It feels good to get this off my chest like a form of best friend therapy. I can't believe how quickly this all took place and I can see it for what it was—a fling. For a hot second, I thought we could be more, but I was stupid.

"Girl," she rolls the R with extra effort. She means business. "That sounds like it belongs in a romance novel! I can't believe someone so business smart can be this dense. I would have walked up to them both and punched them in their faces!"

"I can put it behind me and never have to see him again." I look down at my kitchen table. "If he's smart, he'll just leave me alone, and I won't have to see him at the caffé anymore."

"Are you sure you feel like this is all okay or are you trying to put on a front? Look up at me, missy." She waits until I lift my gaze back to the screen. "Do you want me to show up in Italia and kick this dude's ass? What about the supermodel? I'm sure I could take them both."

I laugh. "I love you, Sophie. No, you don't need to come kick anyone's ass. But if you do want to come here just to visit me, that would be awesome."

"I might have to plan that out!"

Just then, a loud knock at my door startles me. It's a Sunday morning and since I've been in Italy I've only had one visitor ... Leo.

"Sorry, Sophie, I've got to go. Someone's knocking on my door."

"Okay, Elena, don't let that bastard make you sad. You can do better than a guy who would kiss someone else when they've got you by their side. I love you, girl!"

"Love you, too, Soph!"

"*Ciao, ciao.*"

When her face disappears from my screen, I already long to see it again.

By the time I get to the front door, the knocking has turned into pounding. My old wooden door is about to fall off its hinges. There must be a maniac on the other side.

"Elena!" Leo shouts. "Open the goddamn door!"

I've never heard him raise his voice like this before.

"Just go away!" I shout back through the door. "Can't you take a hint? I don't want to see you ever again."

Now, normally, I do not get loud with people. I am the master of the silent treatment. This never upset my past boyfriends because usually when it got time to fight or argue, they were getting ready to end things.

"Elena, so help me! I will break down this door if you don't open it right now!"

Before my neighbors call the police, I throw open the door.

"What?" I end up face-to-face with a furious Leo. His eyes are bloodshot, his hair looks like he's been running his fingers through it all night, and he is still wearing last night's club outfit.

"Where the hell did you go last night?" He pushes his way into my apartment. "You had me worried sick! If the sleazy bartender didn't tell me he saw you leave, I would have called the police thinking you got kidnapped by Russians or worse!"

He paces back and forth through my open kitchen and living room.

"Listen, Leo, I appreciate your concern, but you don't have to worry about me." I remain standing by the door. "I can take care of myself. I didn't want to be there, so I left."

"Why did you leave? And why did you turn your phone off?" He lowers his voice and his shoulders slump.

Did he stay awake all night?

I really don't want to have this conversation with him, especially with him giving me puppy dog eyes. I'm the one who should be shouting.

I just wish he wasn't here and none of this was happening. Why couldn't he just forget about me? He clearly had no problem doing that in the club last night.

"Leo, I saw you," I whisper, looking him dead in the eye.

He squints at me. "Saw me ... what?"

"Saw you making out with that supermodel whore, Aurora Rossi."

"Elena." Leo runs his hands through his hair.

He hasn't denied anything yet.

"Your friends are right." I open the door again. "I'm not good enough to be with you. I'm also not good with watching you being 'friends' with other women right in front of me. Why waste my time and yours? Get out and let's pretend this whole thing never happened between us."

"Elena, I'm sorry you saw that."

That's it? That's the worst apology, ever.

It's driving me insane that he's not even denying it or giving me that "It's not what it looked like" bullshit excuse most men pull out of their asses.

"I thought we were together."

"We are together, as friends. We talked about this, Elena. Aurora was not even invited to the party. Victoria told her it was happening and she crashed." Leo picks up the pacing again. "I was waiting for you to come out of the bathroom and she spotted me. We were talking and then she kissed me. I got caught up in the moment. It was just a quick kiss, anyway."

My jaw drops. "Are you kidding me? You basically told the entire room that you don't even give a fuck about me by kissing someone else with me there. I know you think we are friends, but I feel like you cheated on me."

I try to ignore the tears that want to slide down my cheeks. I can't decide if I'm pissed or heartbroken about his careless explanation.

"Please, listen to me." He steps closer and makes an attempt to grab my hand.

"Don't touch me!" I scream in his face. "I don't want your hands anywhere near me."

He looks like I've just punched him in the gut. I don't think he realized just how serious I was until now. I will not tolerate another person cheating on me. I have flash backs to when I caught Zack in bed with this secretary.

"I'm so sorry, Elena. I didn't cheat on you, *cara*. I am not technically your boyfriend."

And just like that, I'm the one who feels like I've been slapped across the face.

He's trying to get off on a technicality?

"Are you fucking kidding me?" I feel like I scream at him, but it comes out as barely a whisper.

"Elena, please can we put this behind us. I don't see why this is such a big deal. We didn't talk about our boundaries before. Now I know." He takes a step back to give me space. "I didn't go out of my way to kiss Aurora and I definitely did not want you to see that."

"Is this what life will be like with you?" I burst into tears.

I'm picturing myself at future parties with Leo and seeing women all around him, and I can't face this again. I'm not cut out for 'friends with benefits' especially if I have to be worried that Leo will be getting *benefits* from other people.

"*Cara*, please don't cry." He reaches his hand to wipe away my tears, but I flinch as he comes closer and he stops in his tracks.

The tears flow down my face, and I'm to the point where I need a tissue.

"I'm sorry but I can't do this. Leo, please just go. I realized seeing you kissing her that I am not cut out for *this*" I point in between us.

"You don't mean this." His eyes plead, and he steps closer to me. "Give me a chance to make this better."

"I'm sorry, Leo. We both know we weren't meant to be anyway. This would have ended eventually. Let's just get it over with now before it hurts even more." I point toward the open door. "Just go."

He looks me up and down one last time, probably realizing he's not giving up much, and walks out the door.

11

Two weeks without Leo in my life and I can't sleep without tossing and turning. My mind drifts to thoughts of him. I've thrown myself into work and I have to say I have a few desserts under my belt, or should I say apron now.

Marco is even surprised at my baking skills. However, I'm taste testing a few too many of these goodies my jeans are feeling a little snug. I need to visit my dear friend Alessandra at the gym soon.

"Elena, dear. Aren't you looking *bella* today?" Signora Lucca walks up to the counter with a tall man with short, dirty blonde hair and chestnut eyes.

"Buon giorno, Signora Lucca. Grazie." Sadly, I'm not in the mood for whatever this is about to be.

She extends her hand toward the man beside her. "I wanted to introduce you to my doctor, Carlo Romano."

"Nice to meet you, Dr. Romano." I look up at him.

He has an intense gaze on me. I get the feeling I'm being sized up.

"You can call me Carlo. It's great to meet you, Elena. *Signora* Lucca has spoken very highly of you." Gone is the gaze, instead, he flashes me a nice smile.

"Oh, *Signora* Lucca, she stretches the truth." I laugh. "Believe half

85

of everything she's said about me." Not wanting to continue this awkward small talk, I take their coffee orders and get to work on her latte and his cappuccino.

"Well, she got one thing right," Carlo says as I hand him his drink. Signora Lucca hovers by the front door. She's up to no good, that's for sure.

"What's that?"

"She said you were *bella*."

I spill a little of the milk I was pouring into their drinks and I grab a napkin to clean up my mess. I'm not on top of my game, at work or with men, right now.

"*Grazie* to you both. These are on the house."

Signora Lucca winks and gives a little head nod in the direction of the doctor. He is a very attractive man I will give her that.

"I would love to see you again, that is, if you aren't already seeing someone."

"No, I'm single," I say a little too quickly. Great, now he's going to think I'm desperate.

Smooth move, girl. Way to act hard to get.

He hands me his business card as he tells me to call him when I get a break to set something up.

When they are long gone, Marco comes up behind the counter ready to change shifts.

"Did you just get set up by a middle-aged mother?" Marco peeks over my shoulder at the business card. "When is someone going to walk in here and ask me on a date?"

"Marco, be serious. Like you have time to go out on a date with anyone. You are practically married to this caffé."

"You are right. Stella is my *bambina*."

"All right, crazy man, I'm going to leave you with your baby and I'm going to kick my own ass at the gym."

Let's just hope my ex Italian lover is no longer frequenting this gym location.

———

"Ciao, bella! Get your tight ass in my class right now!" Alessandra shouts when I walk into the gym.

I'm glad she's here to keep my mind off the last time I was in the gym, with Leo. This place brings back memories of his chiseled body glistening with sweat.

Why do I have to have such a great memory?

I drop off my bag and jump into the routine as the class is warming up. Alessandra's classes are the best. She pumps the music loud, dims the lights, and has the best choreography. After an hour of an ultimate sweat fest, I don't think I can even feel my muscles anymore. I am spent.

"Hey, wait up!" Alessandra runs to catch up with me as I head to the steam room.

"I haven't seen you in a few weeks. What's new with you, Elena?"

"Just the usual. I've been working at the caffé a lot."

"Come on, you really want to talk about work?" We both strip off our workout clothes and wrap towels around our bodies. "Tell me the juicy stuff! I saw you leave the club on my birthday with the very handsome Leonardo Forte. I didn't know you were friends ... or more based on the way you two had your hands all over each other." She clicks her index fingers together; the Italian hand gesture for having sex.

It makes me a little sad to remember the old days when Leo and I couldn't take our hands off each other. Well, that was just two weeks ago.

"I'm not holding back on any juicy stuff, don't worry. Leo and I were friends, but not anymore."

"Why not? He's a hunky piece of man candy!"

"Man candy or not, he's not really my type."

"You mean an extremely good looking rich man isn't your type?" She laughs.

I take a seat on a long bench and Alessandra sits beside me. "I just don't think we would have wanted the same things in the long run, you know? He dates supermodels and he isn't looking for marriage."

"I can understand not wanting to be with a man who doesn't want marriage, especially if you do, that is. But I wouldn't let the model thing stop you. Beauty fades."

"Well ... I was at his birthday party with him and I caught him kissing Aurora Rossi when I went off to the bathroom."

"What?"

"Yep, you heard me. Super embarrassing. I'm trying to put the entire thing behind me."

She pulls her long blonde ponytail up into a high bun. "I can't believe it. I know from the papers he's normally a player. But the way he was looking at you at the club, he definitely had eyes for you ... and only you."

I blush, thinking about what Leo and I did that night in the private room. My hopes were set too high. I already wanted more than he could give.

"Okay, enough about me. What have you been up to? Let me hear your boy drama."

She shots me a look. "I don't let boys cause drama in my life."

"How is that possible?"

"I don't let them get close enough to me to cause any drama. I use them for what I need and let them go."

"It's that easy?"

"*Sì*, I don't let men rule my life."

That sounds like just the kind of life I should live.

"You should write a rule book or something." I adjust my towel as it nearly slips from my skin. "A lot of girls want your attitude, but a little thing called emotions gets in our way."

She laughs. "You American girls with your big dreams of surprise proposals on bended knee and huge weddings. You know how many girls have Pinterest wedding boards but aren't even engaged?"

Now does not seem like the time to openly admit that I am one of those girls.

"Okay, okay, I get it." I chuckle. "But there's nothing wrong with wanting someone to love you and only you."

I'm a hopeless romantic living in a heartbreak kind of world.

"I agree. Love is special but love doesn't mean you need to run off and get married."

"So you don't want to get married?"

Are all Italians against marriage? Why didn't I know this before I applied for a visa.

"I'll never say never, but it's not a big deal to me."

"You are an aspiring model and you don't want to get married ... you should be dating someone like Leo." The sweat from my head lands on my lap. If I don't leave this sauna soon, I'm going to evaporate.

"Oh no, honey, he's not my type. I don't like men who want someone else in their bed. I don't know what he was doing with that Rossi chick, but the guy I saw in the club wanted you."

Me ... and who else?

———

My dinner date tonight consists of a carry out salad and margarita pizza. Italians really know how to do their pizza. I'm basically ready to eat all the carbs back I burned at the gym.

I grab my laptop and throw on a binge worthy Netflix drama. As I catch myself drifting to sleep, my iPhone rings. I don't recognize the number and normally wouldn't answer, but I've got nothing else to do, so I pick up.

"*Pronto*," I say.

"*Pronto*, Elena! It's Carlo. I'm glad to hear you are answering your phone like a true Italian." His boisterous tone cheers up my grumpy mood.

"How are you, Carlo?"

"I'd be better if a beautiful woman would say she'd go out to dinner with me Friday night."

"Are you trying to ask me to find you a beautiful woman?" I say, playing coy.

"No, *you* are that woman."

Looking from my pizza, Netflix, and sweatpants, I acknowledge that *anything* is better than solitude.

"Well, you've twisted my arm, I guess I should say yes."

"*Bravo*! I am so happy to hear that. I am not 'playing it cool' as you Americans say, am I?"

I laugh at his dorky confession. "Don't worry about it. I'm excited, too."

"I will pick you up around 8 o'clock. Text me your address."

We say our goodbyes, and I hang up the phone.

Am I ready for this?

I'm doing it again. Making a simple dinner something bigger than it should be. This isn't an invitation for a life together, it's just a date.

How could one dinner hurt? At least *Signora* Lucca will get off my back.

———

The next morning I'm at Stella's making chocolate chip cannoli before we open. My thoughts float in the clouds, as usual. I'm getting good at this baking thing when I hear a sound behind me.

Before I can even turn around to check it out, Leo's massive body traps me against the table. His arms surround me and his hot breath is in my ear.

"Leo, what are you doing here?"

"Ssh," he whispers. "Enjoy the moment."

"We really shouldn't be doing this here. I mean, pastries and everything."

Leo does not reply. Instead, he spins me around and plants a deep, caressing kiss on my lips. A small whimper escapes my mouth. I should fight him off, but I can't pull myself away.

Leo takes off my apron and unbuckles my jeans.

I help move the process along quicker and slide them down my legs and reach for his belt. He grabs my hands to stop me and then pushes my panties to the side.

He plunges two fingers deep inside me and uses his thumb to circle my clit. I bite down on his tan neck, holding back my urge to scream. He pumps his fingers in and out, and then takes my juices and rubs it around my clit.

My climax builds as he claims my mouth once again with his. Gently sucking on my bottom lip. I can't hold back. The orgasm rips through me and I climax on his hand.

90

Before I can regain my composure, he spins me back to facing the table and then pushes his huge cock inside me. My panties are still on, and the combination of him slamming hard into me and the fabric rubbing against my clit feels glorious.

"Harder," I growl as I grab on to the table in front of me, holding on tight.

"Come for me," he barks, before thrusting faster.

BEEP BEEP BEEP

My alarm goes off on my phone and I jolt awake. I'm still on the couch, and it was all a dream.

It felt real.

And I wanted it to be real.

1 2

Tonight is date night with Carlo.

Friday came quicker than I thought it would with the coffee shop keeping me busy. Marco let me pitch him a few marketing ideas I've had including setting up social media accounts for Stella's and hosting poetry or open mic nights.

Even though he hasn't asked or pressured me, he's letting me add little bits of my past life into the caffé.

However, even with all the work I've been doing, my dream about Leo always runs in the back of my mind. I've picked up double shifts every day because Marco is doing all he can to right the wrongs his *nonna* made with the business side of things.

"All right Marco. It's 6 o'clock, and I've got to go home to get ready for my date." I place my apron in the drawer.

"The hot date with the doctor! Be sure to remember everything so when *Signora* Lucca comes in here you can give her a play by play."

I roll my eyes. "Real funny. And no one said this was a *hot* date." I shove his arm.

"Abuse!" He grabs his arm in a dramatic show. "I'm going to call the bosses and get you fired."

"Yeah, right. You need me here."

"You're speaking the truth, Elena. Listen, I think of you like a little sister. You are a hardworking person with a good heart. Don't go on dates because you think they will make someone else happy, do it because you want to."

He always seems to speak the truth. Marco is my Yoda—the wise one.

"Thank you, Marco." I give him a quick hug. "You are the older brother I never wanted ... kidding." I laugh. "Tonight is purely for fun to get me out of my apartment so I don't have to watch another Netflix marathon."

"Okay, I believe you. But did you finish *Sons of Anarchy?*"

"Yes! I wouldn't be going out with doctor boy if I was still seeing Jax Teller on the side."

"Elena, you are too much. Now get out of here before you are late for your date."

He practically shoves me out the door.

———

Reminding myself not to have high hopes, I swing open the door to find Carlo waiting in the hallway of my apartment complex.

"You look great," Carlo says. He thrusts a bouquet of lilies toward me. "These are for you."

"Thank you!" I take the flowers from him." You don't look so bad yourself." I wink.

Carlo leans in for a double cheek kiss.

I quickly place the lilies into a vase of water, and we head out to a restaurant in the heart of downtown called *Amore*.

The vibe screams romance with the dim lighting and flowers hanging from the ceiling. Every couple leans in together over candlelight at their small tables.

I imagine everyone is whispering sweet nothings into each other's ears.

This is intense for a casual first date—couldn't we have gone to Italy's version of a Pizza Hut? Really, anything that doesn't scream 'lovey-dovey.'

We're seated at a table near the back of the restaurant, and just like a true gentleman, Carlo pulls out my chair. His hand grazes my lower back as he pushes in toward the table. I'm not quite sure I want him touching a place so intimate just yet, but I decide to ignore it.

The date goes smoothly but it's not too exciting. We talk easily about typical first date conversations and questions—getting to know you stuff. Carlo is polite and makes me laugh as we sip our wine and eat our many Italian courses—from an appetizer of bruschetta to gnocchi, glazed roast, and then a fresh garden salad.

As we wait for our desserts to arrive, I excuse myself to go freshen up in the ladies room.

On my way back to the table, that recognizable hideous laugh halts me dead in my tracks.

Is this what déjà vu feels like?

Before looking where the laugh was coming from, I know whom it belongs to ... Victoria.

From the corner of my eye, I spot her with Leo looking cozy at a table for two. Her leg is running up his from under the table. As I've been torturing myself without him, this man has been adding more notches to his bedpost.

From me to Aurora to Victoria, this man moves quicker than I thought.

Victoria puts her hand on top of his while anger mixed with sadness consumes me. I know I am standing in the middle of the restaurant gawking for too long when Leo looks up from his food and locks eyes with me.

Quickly turning away, I high tail it back to my seat.

I approach the table a little too forcefully as the plates shake.

"Is everything okay, Elena?" Carlo steadies his *tiramisu* plate. "You look upset."

"Everything is perfect, thanks for asking." I brush my hand along with his on top of the table. *Why am I doing this?* I don't want to lead him on—he seems nice but a desperate part of me wants to show Leo that I too can move on quickly.

I dig into the tiramisu waiting for me at the table. It's to die for. I refuse to learn how to make this dessert because then I would probably eat it every single day.

Carlo clears his throat loudly.

Oh, my gosh, was he talking to me?

"I'm sorry." I look up from my cake. "What did you say?"

"I just said you make a little moan when you eat something. It's adorable."

Heat enflames my cheeks.

Why does every Italian guy keep pointing this out? And how do I stop myself from doing it?

"That's not the only thing that makes her moan."

Leo.

He said it quietly, so only I'd hear him but embarrassment, and now anger, rises inside of me.

"*Scusi*, did you say something, *signor?*" Carlo asks Leo.

"*Mi dispiace.*" Leo extends his hand to shake Carlo's. "My name is Leonardo Forte, and I am a friend of your gorgeous date here."

"Nice to meet you, *Signor* Forte. I'm Dr. Carlo Romano."

I sit and stare, not saying a single word. I even put my fork down from my beloved tiramisu. Why couldn't Leo stick to his side of the restaurant cozying up to Victoria?

Has he slept with her?

I should not care about this answer.

Both men are now staring at me. It's safe to say I'm here with the two hottest guys in this place.

"What?" Again, I missed what was asked of me.

"Elena, I just asked your *friend* Carlo here if I could have a word with you ... *privately.*" Leo's intense stare leads me to believe he can see through to my deepest secrets and hear my inner thoughts.

If he could, he'd know I was screaming at him to go away.

"Elena, you don't have to go with him if you don't want to," Carlo says.

Poor Carlo, it's probably hard to read the hot-and-cold dynamic between Leo and I. He doesn't understand what's going on between us, but I'm sure everyone in this restaurant can feel the tension. #Awkward

"No. I'm sorry, Leonardo, but I don't want to talk to you privately ... or ever again." I nod in the direction of his table, where Victoria is still sitting. "You shouldn't keep your *lovely* date waiting."

Leo remains silent for a second too long, and it sets me on edge. His eyes are dark and his strong jaw locks into place.

He's not happy with my answer, which makes me happy.

"As you wish, *cara*." Leo nods at Carlo and then walks away from our table.

When he's out of earshot, Carlo leans over. "That was *the* Leonardo Forte, right?"

Don't tell me he's about to fan girl all over Leo like everyone else seems to.

"That's the one."

Carlo nods. "How do you know him?"

I scoop a piece of tiramisu up onto my fork. "He's just a customer at the coffee shop."

The rest of the date goes on uneventfully and we ignore the fact that we were rudely interrupted and pick up the conversation.

We finish the evening with after dinner macchiatos. I give Carlo a quick kiss on the cheek as he drops me off at my door. We say goodnight and part ways.

It's sad to admit but seeing Leo was the most memorable part of my entire date with Carlo.

———

"Elena," I hear my name from the back of the coffee shop. "Is Elena here?" *Signora* Lucca asks Marco from the front counter.

The last thing I want to do is recap my date from the other night with her. She's like the Italian Patti Stinger from the *Millionaire Matchmaker* but older and nosier.

Contemplating whether or not I should hide out here waiting, I know I need to face the music. Marco is an awful liar, and I don't want to put him in that spot.

"*Buon giorno, Signora* Lucca!" I'm as chipper as I can be as I join Marco behind the counter.

"I'm so happy you are here. How was your date with Carlo?" she asks, with a huge smile on her face. She has high hopes for us, and I feel bad for having to let her down.

"I had a great time, *Signora* Lucca. Carlo was a perfect gentleman—he took me out to a nice dinner."

"And ...?"

"And ...?" I repeat the question back to her.

"Did you invite him in after your nice dinner?" She winks.

"No!" I laugh. "I don't think Carlo and I are on that same page. He was very nice, but I'm not ready to date anyone seriously at the moment."

"Oh, Elena, I'm sorry to hear that." She claps her hands together as if to pray. "I think you two would make a great pair—when you are ready, dear."

Did that really just happen? She let me off the hook easier than I thought she would. I knew that I always liked Signora Lucca. Even though she's been overbearing when it came to going on a date with Carlo, she has my back knowing I'm not ready.

"*Grazie*! I knew you'd understand."

"Of course." She takes her coffee from the counter. "But I will say that, with a beautiful face like yours, if I was your age, I would be ready to date every night!"

Again with this reminder.

I laugh, she laughs, and we all pretend I'm not losing my mind.

Marco and I go about our shift as usual serving customers, making espressos, cleaning the shop, laughing with the regulars, and keeping the pastries flowing. It's not until after the lunch rush of over-caffeinated Italians dies down that I hear the sound of red-soled Christian Louboutins click click clicking across the tile floor.

Looking up to see none other than bitch face Victoria striding toward me.

My good day has been brought to an end ... and what a way for it to die.

"*Ciao*! Welcome to Stella's, what can I get for you?" Marco greets the cold looking Victoria as I try to decide do I run to the back or face the monster head on?

"I'll take a double espresso macchiato."

No "hello" or "please"—go figure she'd be rude to people she thinks are below her. Didn't anyone ever tell her you don't treat the people who deal with your food (or coffee) like shit? Guess not.

"No problem," Marco says.

Marco begins making her drink when she spots me. She takes her huge sunglasses off and stares at me like she's seeing through to my soul.

At least mine isn't black on the inside.

"*Ciao,* Elena." Victoria waves her hand at me as if she were swatting away a bug. "I didn't realize this was the *little* caffé you worked at."

Get real.

Leo has been photographed in this caffé more times than I can count.

I'm 100 percent sure she'd be the kind of crazy girlfriend to keep tabs on him. She probably has some kind of Google Alerts set up to track his every move. She knew this was my coffee shop from the minute she walked in.

"*Ciao,* Victoria. Yes, Stella's is the best!" I say with a super fake smile plastered on my face.

Marco gives her the drink, but she lingers at the counter after paying.

"I saw you at the restaurant on Friday. Were you on a date?"

Looks like I won't be getting out of this conversation easily.

"Oh, I didn't realize you were there," I say. "I was out with a new friend."

Didn't know she was there? That was the best I got?

"Your date looked," she purses her lips together, "cute. I told Leo he didn't have to take me out, but he insisted. You know how he can be when he wants to charm *his* girl. We were celebrating."

My hands clench into tight fists under the counter.

Celebrating what? She wants me to take her bait, but I won't do it.

"Well, that's lovely. I hope you had a great time, you frigid bitch."

Okay that's what I wish I said, but it comes out more like, "Oh, great. I hope you ... um ... had a good time."

Truthfully, I hope she stubs her toe on the way out of the coffee shop. Falls on her face and breaks her teeth.

She bites her bottom lip. "Oh, we *definitely* did. Before and after dinner." Then she winks.

Stop it! Stop it! Stop it! I do not want to hear this.

Yes, I let Leo go, but that doesn't mean I want to hear or think about him with any another woman. Especially the Ice Queen Victoria. I can't believe he had sex with her! I must not have meant as much as he said if he so quickly replaced me.

It was hard for me to go on a date with someone else so soon; I can't even think about having sex with someone else already.

"Good for you two." Picking up a rag, I wipe the counter. "Now if you'll excuse me, I need to get back to work."

I hurry out from behind the counter and into the back room like a coward. I don't want to see her again or have anything to do with her. #MeanGirl

After a few minutes, Marco finds me in the back room sitting on the counter, eyes closed, doing some meditative breathing in a lame attempt to collect my thoughts.

She shouldn't have been able to affect me the way she did.

"You want to talk about it?" he asks me, with a concerned look on his face.

"Nothing really to talk about. That's Leo's new girl ... or maybe latest girl. He moves quickly I've noticed."

"He's definitely downgraded."

"You are too nice, Marco."

Marco takes a seat on an overturned bucket. "Are you kidding? That woman looks evil just by the way she walks. She seems standoff-ish. Like she'd be mean to a puppy."

I don't know what it is about what Marco said but I can't stop laughing! He hit her description right on the point she does look like someone mean enough to not like puppies. Letting out this deep belly laugh feels good to my soul. I haven't laughed like this in weeks, since Leo and I were together.

"Okay, I know I'm no comedian. It wasn't that funny! Did something get lost in translation?"

"*Grazie*, Marco! You know just the right words to say—in any translation."

As I'm wiping away the tears from laughing, we hear the ding of the door chime to let us know a last minute customer has come in.

I walk around the counter and my jaw drops.

"Elena Scott in an apron ... baking. What in the world? You've changed best friend, you've changed." Sophie, who is supposed to be in Michigan, is standing in Stella's.

If she wasn't carrying her luggage, you'd never know this woman just got off a plane. Sophie's long blonde hair is pulled up in a high ponytail and her blue eyes light up her face. I didn't realize how much I missed her until this very moment.

"Sophie, what the heck are you doing here?" I shout.

"I think *ciao* is what you mean to say," Sophie says.

We embrace in a long hug and talk a million miles per minute trying to catch up.

"What's with all the excitement out here?" Marco comes out from the back room and spots us.

"Marco! This is my best friend, Sophie. Sophie, this is my boss, Marco."

I make the introductions and they double kiss each other's cheeks. I notice their eyes linger for a minute too long for a friendly 'hello' but I let it go.

I'll have to tease Sophie about this later.

"So what's the plan for tonight girl? Show me this ridiculously amazing city!"

"Sophie, it's been a crazy day today." I glance at my watch and realize it's not even late. "I'll tell you about it over some pizza and wine. Would you mind staying in tonight? I promise you a fun trip after tonight."

"Wine and pizza? I'm in."

Boy, do I have a lot to catch her up on.

———

After a night of wine, pizza, and girl talk I wake up refreshed. I think getting out all of my feelings, crying on Sophie's shoulder, and then laughing my ass off was good for my mental heath.

Looking over at my snoring friend, I decide to let her sleep in while I practice my culinary kills.

"What's that smell?" Sophie asks as she walks into the kitchen. "Belgian waffles and Americanos. Please tell me you're hungry?"

I sit a plate down in front of her.

"Starving! And very impressed. My Elena had no idea how to use her own microwave, let alone whip up something that smells delicious."

"If you're just going to make fun of me this whole trip, you can get your butt back to Detroit."

"That was cold girl, cold. So what's on the agenda for today?"

And just as Sophie starts to quiz me, there's a loud knock at the door.

Sophie gives me a curious look as I head over to open the door.

"Elena, let's get this trip started!"

Alessandra struts in carrying an overnight bag and looking drop dead gorgeous even this early in the morning. If she wasn't my friend, I'd be jealous.

"You must be Sophia. It's nice to meet you, I'm Alessandra. Any friend of Elena's is a friend of mine," she says as she pulls Sophie into a big bear hug.

It touches me that my two worlds are blending together.

"It's so nice to meet you! What, are you a model? You are freakin' hot! And is anyone going to tell me what's going on?" Sophie says.

It doesn't escape me that these two together should be called the 'blonde beauties'—both of them have long blonde hair and blue eyes.

"We are going to Verona and Milan," I say to Sophie as I clean up our plates. "Grab your bag because we've got a train to catch."

13

We find a pair of seats facing each other, me next to Sophie and Alessandra directly across from us. We settle into reading gossip mags (skipping over the articles about Leo, of course), listening to our iPods, and napping.

After we've been on the train for about two hours, Sophie catches me off guard and pulls out her iPad, asking to run some numbers by me.

I shoot her a death stare that says 'shut up' but she doesn't seem to catch it and continues talking about our current clients.

"Are you guys coworkers?" Alessandra asks when she sees Sophie explaining our newest client, a high end fashion line, to me.

"Coworkers? I wish! Elena is the big boss lady," Sophie says proudly. "I'm her company's Vice President."

"Your boss? Her company?" Alessandra looks back and forth between us. "I thought she works in a coffee shop?"

The blonde beauties both turn to face me. I sink lower and lower into my seat. Do you think at some point I'll become invisible? Why couldn't this be a magical train on its way to Hogwarts or something? Where's my invisibility cloak?

"Elena, what's going on girl?" Sophie gives me a questioning look. I can tell she's not so happy with me. "Why does she think you only work in the coffee shop?"

"Well," I fiddle with my fingers in my lap, "I am working at a coffee shop while I'm here." I avoid eye contact with Sophie. "It doesn't really matter about any of the rest. I'm in Italy to relax and chill out."

"Girls, spill it! I don't like secrets. We Italians are blunt and honest," Alessandra says, locking her blue eyes with mine.

She looks like she means serious business. I knew my little white lie would eventually come to an end, so I start to explain.

"It's not so much that I haven't been honest, I just haven't given the full truth," I say.

Sophie fake sneezes and I swear I hear her say 'bullshit' under her breath.

"Back in America, I own a large social media marketing firm, nothing too crazy," I confess to Alessandra.

"Okay, quit the shit." Sophie puts the iPad down and waves her hands in the air like a maniac. "Elena does not like to talk about herself. She is a business rockstar. She's listed on Forbes '30 under 30' for successful entrepreneurs, she's built this million dollar company all on her own – Rock Star Media. I'm damn proud of you, and you should be too," she says turning toward me.

My heart swells hearing Sophie's pride describing my accomplishments.

"Elena, that's amazing! Why didn't you want any of us to know?" Alessandra asks.

I guess I can take the invisibility cloak off now.

"I just wanted to fly under the radar in Italy. I didn't want anyone to be my friend for my money or for a connection which was what was happening left and right back home. I wanted to be liked for me, not the 'success' people think I bring them. I couldn't take any more fake friends or worse, fake boyfriends. It's exhausting being on guard all the time," I say, hoping they accept my truth.

"I believe you," Alessandra says, picking up one of the magazines and holding it out. "I wouldn't want to see you in here either."

"I'm surprised Leo never said anything—you really think he doesn't know who you are?" Sophia chimes in.

"Why would he? I don't think we are on the same level," I spit out.

But before I can finish my thought both girls turn back to give me a 'shut up bitch' look.

"Okay now that that's out of the way, let's have some fun!" Alessandra says as our train stops.

I can't tell you how much I've needed this day. Shopping and sightseeing in Milan were incredible. I somehow let both Alessandra and Sophie talk me into buying some gorgeous outfits and the shoes, oh my god, the shoes are to die for. #Shopaholic

We are back at the Armani Hotel Milano and getting ready for a night on the town. With these two I feel like I'm going to be in trouble.

I let Alessandra pick out my outfit for the night a tight red bandage dress paired with nude heels. Sophie does my hair in long curls swept to one side. They are both wearing little black dresses and Valentino stilettos. I have to admit, my friends are hot.

We decide to go to a popular club to dance the night away. We make it to the club and, of course, it's packed, but Alessandra knows the bouncer who lets us right in.

At the bar I ask for my usual vodka and Red Bull while the girls place their orders. The music blares loudly and we all head out to the dance floor to shake our groove thangs. I love the feeling of being surrounded by people who are dancing.

As we all move to the latest Ke$ha song, someone places their hands on my hips. I didn't go to many clubs back in the States, I was too busy building an empire, but I know that men grabbed women like the guys do here in Italy.

I quickly spin around to tell the slimeball to get lost but I find myself face-to-face with Carlo.

"Carlo! What are you doing here?" I shout into his ear over the loud music, surprised to find a doctor here.

I'm still aware that his hands are on my hips. He's much more daring than the charming doctor who took me to a nice restaurant and then kissed my cheek sweetly goodbye.

"Elena! You look absolutely *bella*. I'm here with some friends after a work conference." He pulls me closer to keep dancing.

I try not to let my mind get caught up in this moment. I remind myself I'm a single lady and it's not a big deal to just dance with a guy who you know. I don't need to read into anything.

We dance for a few more songs with the girls, all hot sweaty bodies grinding together, and when I feel like I need a breather, I excuse myself to go up to the bar.

"Can I please get a water?" I ask the bartender with her enormous breasts practically shoved in my face. Without a word, she hands me the water and continues to flirt with the guy standing next to me.

I'm chugging my drink when Carlo's hot breath assaults my neck.

"It's a very nice surprise to see you here. This trip was boring before running into you," Carlo breathes into my ear.

"It's fun to see you again too!" I shout over the loud noise, unsure if he can even hear what I'm saying.

"Do you want to take that water and come sit at our table?" He nods his head in the direction of a table with stuffy looking guys. I'm guessing they're all doctors who feel completely out of their element; I don't blame them.

My feet are absolutely killing me so I take him up on his offer.

Carlo guides me toward the booth with his hand pressed into my lower back. Unlike Leo's strong, confident hands, Carlo's feel clammy and grabby.

Why am I even thinking about Leo in a time like this? *Because you miss him.*

Because you miss the things his hands could do to you.

"Gentlemen, this is the gorgeous Elena Scott," Carlo introduces me to the fellow doctors and I take a seat.

Everyone seems very friendly but with the loud music it's hard to get to know anyone, so I just sit and smile while slipping off my heels to rub my feet under the table.

As I slip my shoes back on ready to stand up, Carlo's wandering hand rests on my upper thigh.

Do I want his hand there?

My head spins and it's not from the alcohol; okay maybe a little from the alcohol, but more so from my conflicted emotions.

105

You want a man who didn't want you and now you don't want this man who does.

Carlo takes the hand that's not roaming my leg and cups my chin, turning my face directly at him. His chestnut eyes are trained on my mouth and he hungrily takes possession. His kisses start softly, but quickly he gains his courage and forces his tongue into my mouth.

His hand on my leg starts to inch closer to my sex and I know for sure I am not going to let this guy touch me like this. We barely know each other.

That's ironic? You let Leo do all kinds of things to you in public more than once

Okay inner thoughts, calm down and stop judging me, you bitch.

"We should stop." I push my hand on his chest, trying to separate us as much as I can in this tight booth.

Carlo looks at me like he wants to cuss me out and I can see the evidence of arousal in his pants.

"You don't mean that." He comes in for another sloppy kiss.

I shove him harder this time, pushing myself up and out of the booth.

"Don't ever touch me again," I say before running away from this table to where I spot Sophie and Alessandra still on the dance floor.

They stand with two extremely good looking men. I swear they look like they belong to Italy's soccer team.

"I was ready to cheer you on for getting over Leo with that cute guy you were with, until I saw him get a little too touchy feely! I was about to come lay the smack down on his ass, but I'm proud you took care of it. Are you okay?" Sophie shouts into my ear as she pulls me into a hug.

"Were you spying on me?"

"Of course, did you think I'd let you slip away with a guy I don't know and not keep an eye on you?"

"Thanks! I went on a date with that guy before." I nod in Carlo's direction. "He definitely had some liquid courage in his system tonight though," I say as Alessandra joins us, ditching her guy. "I'm going to catch a cab and head to the hotel. I'm not in the mood for this anymore."

"No way! We will all go," they both reply.

Man, I love my friends.

———

The sun shines into our hotel room but I don't want to open my eyes. My head pounds from our night out, but I can already hear Sophie and Alessandra laughing in the next room, I force myself to get up and join them.

Sophie is sitting at the breakfast table and Alessandra in the hotel room kitchen making omelets.

"That smells divine." I take a seat next to Sophie.

"We thought you'd never wake up, sleeping beauty," Sophie jokes as she slides over a shot of espresso as well as a plate with an omelet and fruit on it.

"You know you could have woken me up," I say, taking my first sip.

Coffee always hits the spot.

"Yeah right, that's like waking a sleeping bear. We aren't suicidal!" They both laugh.

"Okay okay, I'm not that bad, you bitches. But thanks for the delicious breakfast. You guys ready to head to Verona today? I can't wait to see Juliet's balcony."

"Me too!" they say in unison.

Juliet, another woman unlucky in love.

14

The train ride from Milan to Verona isn't as exciting as our first trip when Sophie spilled my big secret. I spend the time looking out the window and wondering what Leo is doing. Everywhere I look I spot couples holding hands and it makes me miss him.

But I don't have time to daydream about things that won't become reality. Instead, I'm able to catch up on all the business accounts Sophie wanted to show me, and I even ask her about how she could help the caffé.

The first stop for three girls without boyfriends ironically is Juliet's balcony. Walking toward the small courtyard and bronze statue, I stop to look at the love letters lining the walls. Seeing all the testaments of love touches my heart.

Even if I can't find love, it makes me happy to see all these people have.

"How many of these couples do you think have broken up?" Sophie says looking at the same wall as me.

"Wow, you are so romantic, Soph. I can't believe you just said that. If you write your name up here that's supposed to mean your love will be everlasting."

"I'm just kidding!" She laughs and nudges my arm. "But really, how many?"

Ignoring her, I walk by myself toward the bronze statue of Juliet. It's an Italian legend that if you touch the right breast of the statue you'll have good fortune and luck in love.

This poor girl, the metal of her chest is worn bare!

I'm not sure if I believe in superstitions, but with my luck in love I figure it doesn't hurt to get in line to feel her up.

First, the Trevi Fountain and now this; apparently I'll do anything to find someone worth loving me.

I stand on the platform, touch the statue's boob, and as I'm about to step down I notice a small boy standing by himself and crying at the other end of the courtyard. Glancing around, I notice no one is paying him any attention.

I walk toward the corner where the boy is. "Hey buddy, what's your name?" I kneel down to get to his eye level.

I'd guess he's about seven or eight years old, he has dark brown hair and big eyes so green they look like they glow. He reminds me of a baby version of a certain Mr. Beautiful.

He looks up at me with tears in his eyes and says, "I'm not supposed to talk to strangers."

My heart instantly melts for him.

"You know my parents taught me the same thing when I was your age. Did your mom or dad teach you that?" I'm trying my hardest to get any information out of him to find help.

"My mom," he squeaks out in between his sobs.

"What does your mom look like? Maybe we can find her together."

I know by the way he's looking at me he's trying to decide if I'm trustworthy or not.

I must pass his test because he continues, "She has hair and eyes like yours."

Brown hair and blue eyes. Not much to go on here but that's probably the best description I'm going to get from a kid.

"What's her name?"

"Giulia."

I'm so proud of this little boy! So many kids don't know their parents' first names.

"Will you take my hand? I'm going to help you find your mom."

He puts his small hand in mine and we walk toward the exit, past Juliet's wall of love letters. I don't see my friends either, where did they go?

"Giulia!" I shout as the boy squeezes my hand tightly. "Giulia! Giulia!"

A police officer across the street spots me screaming and walks toward us. Before he can approach me, a woman about my age runs up to us frantically, screaming and crying.

The little boy let's go of my hand and runs toward the woman. They embrace in a hug, all tears and kisses.

"Leo! My precious Leo! I turned around and you weren't there. I was so scared!" the woman says to my little buddy.

Did she say Leo?

What are the chances? I always seem to find Leos who quickly steal my heart. Or, maybe the better question: are Leos drawn to me because they need me? Am I drawn to them?

The police officer talks to the mother and son and I turn to walk away in hopes of finding my friends.

"Wait," Giulia says as she pulls on my arm, "thank you so much for taking care of Leo! He says you wanted to help him find me. I can't tell you how scared I was when he wasn't there. You are our angel!"

She pulls me into a hug.

"Elena!" I spin around and see Alessandra and Sophie crossing the street toward us. "There you are."

"We've been looking for you everywhere! What's going on?" Sophie says as she eyes the police.

"Nothing to worry about. Ready to go? I think this weird trip has gone on long enough," I reply, "let's go home."

15

"This is to die for," Marco says as he tastes one of my new bakery creations: chocolate biscotti with chocolate chips dipped in white chocolate. I'm going to call it "Chocolate Overload."

After my shifts are over I've been practicing some new baked good recipes.

We clean up my mess and I push through the swinging door to lock up, and my breath gets caught in my chest.

Leo stands at the counter. This I know is not a dream.

My insides instantly turn to mush, seeing his refined face and gorgeous body draped in a dark gray suit with a dark red dress shirt and tie.

Did he get better looking since I've last seen him?

"Leo. *Ciao.* What are you doing here?" I mumble.

I look around and realize he and I are the only ones standing in the caffé. Where the heck did Marco run off to? Whenever I need him, he's no where to be found.

"Elena, I needed to see you." He rakes his fingers through his hair. "I came by the other day but Marco said you were on vacation. I don't like the way things ended the last time we saw each other in the restaurant. What were you doing with that doctor?"

Why does he care the way we ended things?

And why does he care if I'm with someone else?

He's already under Victoria's sheets, and I'm sure he got under Aurora's too. What does he need little ol' me for?

I laugh. "Leo, you don't have to worry about me. We are adults, and apparently this is a smaller town than I thought. I didn't realize we could run into each other so I was thrown off guard when I saw you. I won't let it happen again."

"I don't want you to be caught off guard when you see me. And I want more than anything to see you again. I miss you. I can't stop thinking about you. I've never missed someone so much. And you haven't answered. What did you do with that doctor?"

Hold up, wait a minute.

He misses me, but Victoria said they were together? And what about Aurora?

Why does he miss me when he has so many women throwing themselves at his feet?

My brain is going to explode with all the questions swirling inside.

"It didn't look like you missed me when you were with Victoria cozied up together, letting her put her hand on your leg." I almost barf at the mere memory.

Leo shakes his head. "Victoria asked me to dinner to discuss a charity event that both of our companies are putting on together. If you looked at the table, you would have seen files and spreadsheets—it was a *business* dinner."

"In a fancy restaurant?" My hands go to my hips.

"That wasn't a fancy restaurant to me."

Oh. #Burn

"Well, what about her hand on your leg?"

"She placed her hand on my leg for one second, and I quickly removed it. I also let her know that there was no way we would be together, ever. She's not my type, and you, of all people, should know that."

"Okay then, what's your type?"

"My type is ... *you*."

He gives me his signature smirk, but I can see that behind his player attitude, his eyes show honesty. My cheeks blush. What is with all this blushing when I'm around him? I used to have a much better control of my emotions ... until him.

"Leo, I don't know what you are getting at, but Victoria was in here before I went on vacation. She told me *you* asked her to dinner to celebrate. She also made it seem like you two were an item and that you are sleeping together."

My eyes search his face for an answer, but he remains calm and emotionless.

"That's not true. Deep down you know that. Just weeks ago you were the one in my bed, and there has been no one since."

My heart jumps for joy.

It was hard to believe that someone like Leo would be with the Ice Queen. He hasn't slept with her—that lying home wrecker!

Why did she say all that stuff? What a low thing to do even for someone like her. But why I am I surprised?

"Can you say the same about not being with anyone since we split up?"

"Leo, I did not sleep with Carlo. I did see him at a nightclub while on vacation and we ... kissed ... but I ended it. I didn't want to kiss him, I wanted to be kissing you."

He walks and cups my face with his warm hands. I've missed these hands.

"Elena, I want you back. Please let me back in your life."

"Leo, I believe you that you aren't with Victoria but I still can't get the thought of you and Aurora kissing out of my head. How can I trust you?" I stare into his emerald eyes.

His hand is still on my face, and he brushes a stray curl behind my ear.

"I know I can't make it all better by promising the right words. You have to let me prove it you with my actions, Elena. Please, give me another chance to make this right."

Tears form in my eyes. Leo brings his lips to gently meet mine but he hoovers there without connecting our mouths—as if asking for permission. I pull him in closer by his suit and crash our mouths into each other. He's like a drug and I'm getting a hit after a major withdrawal.

I suck on his lower lip and then tease his lips with my tongue. He lets out a low growl and pulls me even closer.

I don't know if things will be right between us again, but I know I don't want this to stop. I've missed him so much. No one has ever made me feel this good before ... ever.

Grabbing onto his chiseled arms, I run my hands over his chest. Taking off his tie, I then unbutton his dress shirt.

Leo removes my apron and unzips my black skinny jeans.

"Leo, wait," I say breathlessly as he starts to push my jeans down. "Wait, wait. We can't do this here. Marco could walk in or a last customer. The door is unlocked, and we are standing in the middle of my workplace in front of open windows."

Leo stops what he's doing, looking just as frazzled as I feel.

"You're right." Leo laughs. "We can't do this here. I wouldn't want anyone to see what's mine. I don't share."

He says the last sentence with such force. He's letting the message sink in. I think someone knows how it feels to be on the other end of seeing the person they care about with another.

"I don't share either." I poke him in the chest. "I'm all yours, if you're all mine." I make a point to say it just as strong as he did, even though on the inside I'm uneasy.

I push back from him, and we start to dress ourselves again.

"But wait a second. You don't want anyone else to see what's yours, but we've done very intimate things in public places before."

Leo blushes this time. It's a rare sight but makes him even sexier to me.

"*Cara*, during the other times, I knew no one would notice. I closed off that room at the club, and for my birthday the table was high and draped with a long cloth. This time we are truly ... exposed."

I just shake my head in disbelief. Here he had me thinking I was a wild woman. I head to the back room to do a quick scan for Marco, who I know must have snuck out the back door when Leo walked in.

We walk out the front door together; I lock the door, and Leo stares.

"Did you eat dinner?"

The irony of his question hits me when my stomach grumbles loud enough for the whole block to hear. I can't lie to him now.

"I'll take that as a no." Leo laughs and grabs my hand to lead me to his town car.

He opens the back door, and even with the tinted windows, I know Mateo is in the driver's seat. I plop inside next to Leo, his smell taking over the back seat, having a feeling of déjà vu from our first car ride together in the limo.

We end up at a gorgeous little restaurant just outside of Rome. The drive couldn't have been more than twenty minutes, but it feels like we are in an entirely different place.

It's quiet, the stars shine overhead, and we sit outside where strings of outdoor lights are draped around the trees. There are a few other couples here, but they look just as into each other as Leo and I are.

"This place feels so cozy," I say, picking up my menu—*Armando's Bistro*.

"It's one of my favorites." He places his menu down without bothering to look at it. "I know the owner. Armando was a friend of my father when I was growing up. He's like an uncle to me. He has a very kind family and they all treat me like their own, especially after my father died and my mom withdrew from the world. It was nice to have them with me."

Before I can ask him any more details about his family a young waitress walks up to our table and sets down a breadbasket.

"Bread. You found the way to my heart," I say to the waitress as I pick up a fresh from the oven roll and spread on some butter.

The waitress laughs and Leo introduces her as Armando's granddaughter, Abrianna. She takes our drink orders and then hurries away.

"I didn't know that if I wanted your heart, all I had to do was give you bread," Leo jokes as he takes a roll for himself.

"Yes, bread and sweets! Both could score you some brownie points with me." I wink.

"I'll have to remember that." He locks eyes with me intensely, and then he asks, "Do I need to be scoring brownie points with you, Elena?"

I honestly don't know how to answer. I am not certain about anything anymore. Our relationship feels like it needs a fresh start, but I am certain that my heart does not want this man to be with anyone else.

He is mine.

My stomach hurts just at the thought of someone else touching him, let alone having sex with him or sharing intimate details about their lives together.

But is this good for me? Will he get to the point where the newness has worn off and he gets bored? His friends already clearly hate my guts; maybe they'll have an influence?

And a question I've been trying to avoid: what about when he finds out that I've been lying to him about who I am?

It can't mean that much, can it? But I don't want to bring that information into what we've already got. I do know I'll eventually need to tell him about my own company.

"Elena, you look deep in thought," he leans back in his chair. "Tell me what's going on in that head of yours."

"I wish it were that easy to just lay it all out for you."

"But it can be. Just tell me what has you making that face."

"What face?" I say, sticking out my tongue to break up the seriousness of this conversation.

"I can think of many other places to use that tongue."

I choke on my water. I didn't think this conversation would turn to sex so quickly but, heck, look who I'm talking to. We can't ever seem to get away from our insanely intense physical attraction.

"I don't know how I feel about ... *us*."

"Are you still upset with me?" he says, looking at me with big puppy dog eyes, and I can't help but want to cuddle up in his lap and console him.

"Yes." It's hard for me to say. "And, no. Leo, I'm not upset anymore. Our time apart let me clear my head and I realize just how much I do want you in my life. But I'm confused. I'm unsure about everything." I fiddle with the laminated menu. "I don't know how you feel about me, and it makes me crazy. But I also know that I don't want to be away from you again. I was miserable. And I sure as hell don't want you to be with anyone else. The thought of that makes me want to get sick and angry all at the same time."

I meet his eyes across the table, and he knows I just put my heart on the line for him an honest confession. He reaches across and grabs my hand on top of the table.

"Elena, I will make it so you will never doubt my feelings again. I can't stop thinking about you. It drove me crazy to be away from you for so long and I was also depressed. Then I almost turned into The Hulk at that restaurant when I saw you with another man!"

Leo as The Hulk ... I would love to see him rip his shirt off.

"Maybe we can start fresh?" I ask.

Before he can answer me, Abrianna approaches our table with an older man.

He's shorter and has a round belly, but his face breaks out into a wide smile when he sees us.

"Leonardo, my boy! *Come stai*? I haven't seen you in so long. And who is this young lady? *Molto bella.*"

The man, who I am guessing is Armando, grabs my hand and plants a kiss on the top of it. Leo stands up to embrace him in a hug.

"*Zio* Armando! Sorry it's been so long. I couldn't think of any place I'd rather bring Elena for dinner tonight than your astounding restaurant. I'm so happy you are here to meet her."

The two men talk quickly in an Italian dialect that I do not understand, but watching them is like watching a movie they are very animated. It's quite a show! It makes me happy to meet someone close to Leo like family.

Our dinner of risotto with Gorgonzola and fresh pear sauce followed by pork tenderloin and an house salad ends up being divine. We wash it all down with a sweet white wine and enjoy milk chocolate mousse for dessert.

Man, *Zio* Armando can cook.

The conversation with Leo stays fun and light hearted for the rest of the night. I love taking a break from all the seriousness of our regular conversations and just being able to relax with Leo.

This is the first time since our break up that I've felt my muscles release their tension.

How long will this last?

16

Again, I'm alone in Leo's bedroom.

Looking around the floor, my clothes are scattered every which way. As soon as we got back from the bistro, Leo ripped them off me. #Animal

Letting my body sink deeper into this soft bed, I want to drift back to sleep. Yet my stomach let's me know it has other plans.

I throw my clothes back on and do the walk of shame downstairs to find Gemma in the kitchen.

"Good morning, Elena. Leo went into the office but he left you this note. I'll have breakfast and coffee ready for you in a few minutes."

I take a seat at the marble kitchen table and read Leo's note:

My lovely Elena,

Went into the office to get about an hour of work out of the way so I can spend the rest of the weekend with you.

Your Leo

My Leo.

I love the way that sounds. I put the note down, and Gemma places a plate with Florence style eggs Benedict and an espresso in front of me.

"Gemma, this looks great! *Grazie*," I say with a mouthful of food as I dig in.

"*Prego*. I'm glad you enjoy eating, unlike many of the other women," Gemma says with her back to me as she loads the dishwasher.

"Are there often other women here?"

I wonder how often Gemma is making breakfasts for different women of the week. Truthfully, I should feel bad asking questions behind Leo's back, but I'm too curious.

"No, no, I'm sorry. I didn't mean other women here. I just meant women, in general. Everyone seems to be on a diet," she says as she turns to face me, and I can see she's brushing off the conversation.

"Oh, that makes sense. *Si,* I love to eat." I laugh it off.

There was something hidden behind that comment that I won't forget but for now, I'm not going to prey farther. I finish my meal and excuse myself from the kitchen.

Finding Leo's home gym, I grab a yoga mat and make myself at home. I'm not a fan of the stillness of yoga but in this moment clearing my cluttered mind is just what I need.

I've been moving through sun salutations for about an hour and my body feels calm, present in the moment, and stretched to the max. I've got a slight sweat going as I listen to the calming music from my playlist.

My eyes are closed, and I'm bent over in downward facing dog, hands on the ground and butt in the air. Out of nowhere, I feel hands on my hips and I quickly open my eyes but stay in this position. Through my legs, I see Leo's legs standing behind me.

From this position, I can also see our reflections in the floor-to-ceiling mirrors he has lining the gym walls.

"This is a nice position to find you in,," Leo growls from behind me, "but I'm going to need you to take off these clothes and get back into it."

"I'd say you are wearing too many clothes, as well. Ditch them, Mr. Beautiful."

We strip off our clothes faster than I've ever seen before, and I get back into my downward facing dog position again.

With my butt high in the air like this, I feel very exposed yet turned on.

Leo takes a wide stance and grips my hips with his strong hands. He massages my butt and trails his fingers lightly over my back and legs.

Leo puts his fingers on my sweet spot and strokes me. Electricity courses through my nerves at the simplest touch. "I love that you are always ready for me."

He surprises me when he bites down hard on my butt cheek and then kisses the spot after.

His expert fingers rub my clit until I force my eyes to close or else I might see stars. Before I can beg for him to continue, his cock slips inside of me. I groan out in delight.

My arms burn from holding this downward dog position, but I don't want to say anything. I simply want to enjoy. I sway up and down on my toes, rocking back into his groin.

"Don't stop, Elena." Leo slams into me hard. With his force, I nearly fall forward onto my face but I catch myself.

Continuing to rock back in just the right way this angle hits my G stop. Leo knows I'm ready and he slides his hands around my waist and uses my juices to rub on my clit at the same time as he thrusts.

My brain is about to short circuit itself from the stimulation. There's only one thing my whole body wants.

"Elena, don't come until I say so," Leo commands me as he rubs my clit quicker. I don't know if I'll be able to obey him this time, even if I wanted to.

Leo pulls out, and I'm instantly left with an empty pit in my stomach.

He positions the head of his erection at the entrance of my slick pussy and then slams deep inside, filling me up. I can't take much more, and my arms shake from holding up my body. My legs shake for other reasons.

"Elena, now," he commands as he tosses his head back, and

together we climax and collapse onto my yoga mat. We lay breathlessly tangled in each other for a few quiet minutes.

"We should work out together more often," Leo says laughing.

———

The hot and steamy yoga session is followed up by fun in his magnificent marble titled shower with a waterfall spout. There has to be at least nine shower heads in his bathroom which hit your body in all the right angles. Not to mention the separate clawfoot tub. To die for!

I could live in this bathroom forever, especially if it involves taking long showers with my Mr. Beautiful.

Leo leaves me to get ready as he goes down to his home office to check in on some work. The man is so driven, and his hustle inspires me.

After putting my hair into a long side braid and throwing on a long colorful maxi skirt, white tank top, and wedges, I head downstairs to find my man. Before walking into his home office, I hear Leo on the phone speaking quickly in Italian but I can make out what he is saying.

"I know it's important to you. I can't be at every function you do or I would never get any work done."

With my ear still pressed to the door, it sounds like the other person wants Leo to show up at a charity ball next Saturday night.

Leo lets out a sigh and says, "Okay, okay, Mama. I promise I will attend, put me down for two," there's a long pause, "Yes, I am bringing a date," another long pause, "Yes, I'm sure you'll like her. Okay, *ciao, ciao.*"

When I know it's safe and Leo is off the phone, I walk inside, and he instantly looks up from his laptop and flashes me a devilish grin.

"So ... tell me about this charity ball." I walk around to sit on his desk.

"Eavesdropping is a skill you should add to your resume." Leo pushes his chair back and picks my feet up. He takes off my wedges and rubs my feet in his lap.

"I wasn't eavesdropping so much as waiting for the right moment to walk in. You sounded a little upset on the phone, and I didn't want to make it worse by intruding."

"You could never make anything worse, *bella*."

"So I'm going to get to meet your mom?"

"*Sí*." He digs his fingers into the heel of my foot in just the right way. "This charity ball is for her organization that supports breast cancer research. It's an annual event; she's been throwing it for the last 10 years now, and each year it raises a great deal of money." He transitions his focus to my other foot. I try to keep my focus on what he's saying and not how good this feels. "She suffered a scare a few years after my father passed away and has thrown herself into research to help others."

"Wow. That's incredible she turned her experience around to help others."

Leo nods. "She doesn't always have the kindest heart toward the people she knows personally, but I have to commend her when it comes to giving to charity. She gives both her time and money I did learn a lot from her in that sense."

"Do you think she's going to like me?"

I have only met one of my boyfriends' parents before, and it was by accident. We were making out on his basement couch when they walked in. The surprise was on them and me.

They didn't know they'd catch us in a compromising position,. and I didn't know he live with his Mommy and Daddy. I'm glad his parents stopped us before I had sex with him. Another loser bites the dust.

"I don't care if she does or doesn't." Leo adds more pressure to the foot rub. "Don't doubt yourself, *bella*. You are the best thing that's ever come into my life."

He stares at me, and for a second I think he may say those three little words, but the moment passes when his cellphone rings.

We look at the caller ID displaying Mateo's name.

Leo answers the phone and then sits silently taking in Mateo's words. I can hear the normally quiet man loudly on the other end of line. He's speaking very quickly, and I can only catch a few words, but I swear I hear him say 'stalker.'

Leo does not look as alarmed as I am.

Is Leo being stalked?

Just then he puts his hand over the speaker and says to me, "I'm sorry. I need to take this for work. I should be done in about an hour, and then we can go out to dinner."

I hop off his desk with a pit of fear in my gut. We will need to circle back to this conversation.

Should I be worried about Leo's safety?

With his larger than life persona, has this been something I should have worried about since day one?

17

I'm not sure about this.

I stare at the floor length gown in awe. It's high fashion, sure. But is it for me? I'm not entirely sold.

After dinner, Leo took me shopping down *Via del Corso*.

Picture it: shop after shop of the most luxurious brands in fashion. Scattered amongst the name brands, there are a few small family-owned boutiques.

That's how I found myself in this dressing room trying to find just the right outfit to not only meet Leo's mother but to be photographed as his date for a publicized charity event.

The pressure is on.

I've already tried a few gowns on that got Leo's nod of approval but I wasn't thrilled. I'm not sold on a nod. I want his jaw to drop, his eyes to sparkle, or at least for him to utter a compliment.

Can't a guy tell a girl she's *bella* when she really needs to hear it?

Stepping into the tight maroon sequined dress, I admit it might be a little too short for a charity ball, landing just a few inches above my knees, but once I slipped it on I knew it was my favorite.

Opening the door to the fitting room, I hold my breath in anticipation for another lame head nod.

Instead, Leo's eyes slowly travel up my long legs, taking me all in. The way he looks at me worshipping my body makes me want to straddle him in the store.

"Elena, you look exquisite."

We've found a winner!

"You don't think it's too short?" I fidget with the hem of the dress, trying to pull it down a bit.

Again, his eyes roam over my bare legs.

"Not at all. You have the best pair of legs I've ever seen."

My cheeks must be a shade of rosy red with that compliment.

"Then I'll take it."

I spin back around into the fitting room. Standing in just my bra and underwear, a knock at the door surprises me. Thinking it's the sales lady to check on me, I open the door just a crack to hand her the dress to package up, but instead, a certain handsome Italian man pushes his way inside.

"What are you doing in here?" I whisper. "What is she comes to check on me?"

"Then she'll be in for a show."

Leo's powerful hands lift me up. He presses my back against one of the walls separating us from the other dressing rooms.

"Looks like you are ready." I raise my eyebrows. His rock hard cock is pressing against my lacy panties.

"I want you," he whispers in between hot kisses.

"Wait, wait … put me down," I manage to get out while he devours my tongue.

"*Cara*, I will only put you down if it's a good reason," he whispers again, trying not to attract attention, and my gaze locks to his.

"I need your pants off … now!"

The second he puts my feet back on the ground, I unzip his pants and get on my knees. Sliding his boxer briefs down his legs, his manhood springs out—thick and hard.

Grabbing his shaft with both hands, I spit onto his cock and use my saliva as lube to rub him up and down. He fists my hair with a tight grip.

Twirling my tongue around his tip over and over, his cock pulses in my hands. When he's about to break, I gently massage his balls, one at a time.

Leo hisses a breath that only encourages me to keep going. Replacing my hands with my mouth, I cup his ball in my mouth and roll my tongue around it.

"Oh, *cazzo*," he hisses *fuck* above me.

Yes, enjoy it Mr. Beautiful.

When he has to be at his edge, Leo pulls me up off the ground and spins me around to face the mirror.

I watch with hungry eyes as in a matter of seconds he tosses my bra and panties to the ground.

Standing gloriously in front of the mirror, we are both naked as the days we were born. But the reflection staring back at me is unlike any I've ever seen before.

My lips are swollen, my breasts are heavy and hyper sensitive, and we both have a glow radiating off us.

The air in his room is scented with designer perfume and pure sex. Anyone outside this door has to know what's going on. No longer are we quiet.

"I want you to beg for my cock." Leo wraps his arm around my waist and slides his fingers between my thighs. I'm already wet from thinking about the pleasure I was giving him.

His fingers stroke over my pussy, and I quiver.

"Leo ... please," I grind myself harder into his hand.

"What do you want, Elena?" He stops moving his hand.

"I want you inside of me," I pant.

With his other hand, he pulls my nipples to a hard point. He grips onto my breast and I nearly lose my balance. When I can barely stand, Leo pushes me closer to the mirror.

Placing both of my hands against the mirror, I wait eagerly for Leo to slip his hard cock inside of me. He teases my entrance with the juices between us as I rock back onto him.

"Put your cock inside of me."

This time it's a demand and this time he obeys.

Pushing himself inside my puss, we pound into each other like wild animals.

"Elena, look up at us," Leo commands.

Drifting my gaze away from our bodies to look at our faces, my mouth drops. The pupils of my blue eyes are wider than I've ever seen. Leo's green pair match mine.

He's claiming his prey and I'm ready to be devoured.

Leo diverts his eyes to my tender breasts which bounce upon each hard thrust into my core.

I arch my body back in wanton need. Leo grips the back of my neck and gives it a tight squeeze.

Putting my own hand against my clit, I rub myself which Leo holds onto my neck and pounds into me with his cock. My stomach pulls and with one final slam, we climax together.

He releases my neck, which is red like fire.

Together our skin is damp and flushed. Our breathing is labored as we quickly and quietly put on our clothes.

Before Leo leaves the room, he looks at me and whispers into my ear, "Elena, you better get that dress."

18

Is this what an anxiety attack feels like?

It must be.

My nerves are in my throat, my chest is in pain, and if I leaned over a toilet I'd most certainly throw up. I'm too afraid to do an Internet search of my symptoms. I'm sure I'd find out I have a brain tumor or some sort.

Today is the day of the charity ball.

Even though Leo made it clear he did not care about his mom's opinion of me, I want her to like me.

No, I want her to *love* me.

It would kill me if someone important in Leo's life hated me, especially his mother.

And what if he one day changed his mind? What if he decides to care about his family's opinions?

I've been staying at Leo's home in Tivoli, just outside Rome, every night. We have a routine and it touches my heart how nauseously cute it is. It feels like he's my boyfriend. We get ready side-by-side each morning and then spend our evenings eating Gemma's dinners and curling up on the couch binge watching TV shows on Netflix or playing board games.

When I'm away from him working at the caffè, I miss him. Yes, I've become that girl. There's no further talk about love or marriage though—but I know my heart belongs fully to him.

I've fallen and I've fallen fast.

"Good morning, *bella*." Leo greets me in the kitchen with a kiss on my cheek and a smack on the ass. I'm reading the paper and drinking an espresso standing at the island.

Gemma would be a hit in the coffee shop—her espresso is next level.

"Good morning, Mr. Beautiful." I place the paper at his seat at the table before I sit down.

He shakes his head. Strands of his dark hair fall into his eyes before he brushes them away. "What's with you and this crazy nickname."

Leaning over, I kiss his cheek. "It just feels right."

Leo grabs my hands in his. "Listen, I know you've been stressed about tonight's ball, which you have no reason to be. But to take some of the pressure off, I booked you a day at the spa. Plus, someone will be here to do your hair and makeup."

"Leo, you don't have to do this! I don't want you to spend so much money on me. I can do my own hair and makeup."

"Elena, money is no issue. I want to spoil you and I want you to feel like a queen at the ball. Please, let me do this for you."

Well, no one has to beg me to be pampered. This man is too much. I love how he can sense what I'm feeling and just what I need to relax. Even though he doesn't always address his emotions, I sense how much he cares about me from his actions.

I get up from my seat and climb into his lap, wrapping my arms around his neck. "You always seem to surprise me."

"Well, if I knew this would be how you thank me, I'd surprise you more often."Leo kisses my lips softly. His cock pulses beneath me. His eyes darken.

"*Cara*, before you drive me any more crazy, you need to go get ready to leave. Mateo is waiting outside. Your appointment is in 20 minutes."

Placing my hand over his pants, I kiss his lips before heading a low moan from his mouth. "I want you to think of me while I'm gone."

"You're the one thing always on my mind."

The afternoon at the spa was just what I needed to calm my anxious nerves.

Now I'm getting beautified by the best hair and makeup artists in all of Italy. Leo certainly went all out for me for this event.

"You have the most amazing thick, curly hair, *bella*. You are sure you're not Italian. You are a dream client!" Gino, my new hairstylist, gushes over me.

"No, I don't think there's any Italian in my blood," I laugh.

There's an Italian in my bed every night though.

He spins my chair around, and I look at myself in the bathroom mirror. He's done my hair half up and half down in long curls with a side swept bang. My makeup is a romantic smoky eye look.

Throwing on a diamond bangle bracelet and black Christian Louboutins, I'm ready to go! I thank my fairy gloss mothers for all their help, and I take one last look in the mirror before heading downstairs where I know my man is waiting.

Walking down the long staircase leading to Leo, I spot him staring up at me looking sexy as ever. He's wearing a black slim fit Armani suit with a black button up and maroon tie to match my dress. #Adorable

"You look magnificent." Leo pulls me into an embrace.

"Right back at you, Mr. Beautiful!" I smack his ass.

The ride to the Ruka House Ballroom is short, and I'm proud to say we managed to keep our hands *mostly* to ourselves along the way.

Leo did try to put the moves on me, but I quickly remind him that Gino would kill him if he found out that no one saw how great my hair and makeup looked before I was ravished by my Italian boy toy.

Leo tells Mateo he wants to escort me out of the limo himself. I notice Leo has extra security following us in a separate town car. This reminds me I need to ask him about overhearing his conversation with Mateo the other day, when I thought I heard the word stalker.

Before I can bring it up, Leo turns to me, letting me know that this is a red carpet event and there will be hundreds of cameras ready to take our pictures.

He explains the "step and repeat" process to me, and I pretend I've never been on a red carpet before—that's the life I'm taking a much needed break from. Luckily, he says that since this is his mother's charity event, they'll refrain from making rude remarks to us ... we hope.

You never know what the paparazzi will do or say.

Taking Leo's hand, he holds mine tightly, letting me know he's here to protect me.

I don't have much time to second guess myself.

3 ... 2 ... 1

"Leo! Leo!" The photographers shout as we stop for pictures. "Who's your date, Leo?" They keep screaming.

Leo doesn't answer any of their questions. We simply smile, pose and keep walking.

And that's when I see her. Victoria getting out of a limo with Arturo on her arm. Why are they here?

Leo must have noticed my stance become rigid, and the next thing I know, he dips me, planting an over-the-top kiss on my lips. The photographers go wild! Flash after flash of hundreds of cameras and smartphones record this moment.

"Her name is Elena Scott, and she's my remarkable girlfriend."

His girlfriend!

Be still my heart. I would climb him like a tree right now if we weren't in front of all these people. He called me his girlfriend. I don't know when he made this decision, but I can't get over how good it feels to hear him call me his own. To move past that stupid idea of 'lovers' and be officially an item.

Leo doesn't say anything about the bomb he just dropped on the paparazzi; instead, he plants a kiss on the top of my head and we keep walking the red carpet. We walk hand-in-hand to the entrance of the most striking party I've ever seen.

I didn't know what to expect from a ball, but I can say this blows my imagination out of the water.

Crystals hang from the ceiling on stunning chandeliers in this large white and black ballroom. There's a purple hue to the lighting that creates an romantic ambiance. The tables are lined with the finest china, and violets draped in even more crystals make up the centerpieces. A live band sits on a giant stage near the wall just past a dance floor, which is currently empty because everyone is finding seats and chatting.

What makes the room shine even more than the decor are the guests. This ball makes Leo's birthday bash look like a small backyard shindig with some Italian hillbillies. So many big name A listers and people who look like they bathe in money mingle here.

Leo and I find our table near the stage. Before I can scan the table's name cards, a posh, short woman with short brown hair dressed in a floor length black dress approaches.

"Leonardo, son, you look handsome. I'm glad to see you decided to join us." She kisses each one of his cheeks. "And this must be the one responsible for keeping you away from your mother so much?"

Oh yeah, this is going to be fun.

Leo's mother extends her hand to me in a delicate way. I was afraid I was going to break her but her surprisingly strong grasp lets me know she's a lady not to mess with.

"I'm Elena. It's so nice to meet you." I flash her my best 'American nice girl' smile. She smiles back but her expression looks pained. My father says if a smile doesn't reach their eyes, then it's not genuine. This woman is staring at me with eyes of frost.

I'm familiar with this look from another Italian woman at this ball.

"I'm Rosalie. I'm glad to see you got my son to show up tonight. He likes to avoid events like this."

I notice she didn't say it was nice to meet me, too. This isn't going as well as I hoped. Why did I care if she liked me again? Oh yeah, because I'm hopelessly in love with her son, the man we both happen to have our hands on right now.

"Mama, you know I'd much rather cut a check than come to these events. It's just for show, nothing more."

"How can you say that, Leonardo?" she asks, looking up at him from her small frame. "I live for this charity ball, and it does great things for so many people."

"You know what I mean. Not this event specifically, just events in general. Never mind." He shakes his head.

Did Leo just back down to someone?

He sounded like a teenage boy unsure of himself. Why is he explaining himself to her?

We are still holding hands, and I look up at him to see that he and his mother are just staring at one another, as if they are challenging one another.

And just to make matters even worse, the voice I hate interrupts my thoughts.

"Leonardo, Rosalie, there you two are!" Victoria approaches the small circle we've created. She pushes herself right into the center. "Your ball looks *bravo,* like always. You did a great job."

"Victoria, my darling, I'm so grateful you could come." Rosalie smiles for Victoria does not match the one she gave me. Instead, these two women embrace into a hug.

Victoria and Rosalie are friends. Why didn't anyone tell me? Victoria has her back turned to me and hasn't once muttered a word to me.

You know what? I can be the bigger person here.

"*Ciao*, Victoria. It's nice to see you," I say with a strong voice, head held high.

"Oh, Elena." She turns her rigid body to me. "I didn't even see you there! How do you like your first ball?"

"What do you mean?" I lay it on thick with my Midwestern accent. "I had two meaty Italian balls in my mouth just this morning."

Leo chokes on his own spit.

The joke seems to be lost in translation with Rosalie. However, Victoria's lifeless eyes go wide before she says, "I assume you haven't attended anything as nice as this before."

Again with the white trash jokes?

"You know what they say when people assume," I tease.

Leo laughs and squeezes me hand. He leans down and kisses my cheek. Both women seem taken aback by the public display of affection before they glance away.

We all take our seats, conveniently at the same table and many courses start to make their way over to us.

Luckily for my sanity, Victoria and Arturo are across the table and I can't quite hear them over the noise of the band.

Next to me on my left is Danilo, the owner of the biggest T.V. news station in Italy, and his wife, Gianna. They ask me many questions about life back in Michigan. I fill them in on the bare basics. Luckily they ask mostly about my personal life, not so much about work.

I'm not a good liar so I try to avoid the topic of work in general.

After our appetizers are served, Rosalie gets up to make a speech for all her guests.

"Buona sera, everyone! Thank you for taking the time to join the European Breast Cancer Association and myself for tonight's annual ball. According to the World Health Organization, breast cancer is the most common cancer among women worldwide. It claims the lives of hundreds of thousands of women each year.

"Through the research that the outstanding Association is developing, we have a goal to fight breast cancer and stop it at its early stages. I encourage each and every one of the women here to take steps to schedule breast exams and mammograms. And I encourage each and every one of the men here to talk to the women in their lives about their health.

"Now get out your checkbooks, my friends and family, because I know you aren't cheap. Don't make me look bad the Association needs your help. *Grazie!*"

Everyone claps and Rosalie receives a standing ovation. I'm impressed by how well Leo's mother carries herself in front of everyone. She is still her aristocratic self, but in front of her audience she comes across a bit warmer.

The dinner courses and conversations continue to flow at our table, and I'm having a great time that is, until Victoria opens her loud mouth and her voice carries across the table, piercing my ears.

"Elena, *dearie*, so tell us what you did for a living back in Minnesota. Were you a coffee girl there too?"

Why does she have to go and ruin a great night? Because she's Victoria, that's why, I remind myself.

"Back in *Michigan*, I worked in social media and promotional campaigns."

That's the most basic answer I can come up with that isn't far from the truth.

"That sounds like a lot of fun," Danilo says. "Social media plays a major part in news organizations around the country. Nowadays we can spread stories quicker on Twitter than anything else. I'd love to hear more about your social media work."

I'm grateful for his kind opinion before Victoria has a chance to bring me down yet again.

Leo has his hand on my thigh under the table, and he gives it a little squeeze. His touch calms me down *and* turns me on. Reaching under the table, I place my hand on top of his. I can think of other places I want his hands.

Roaming all over my body.

"So you play on Facebook or something?" Victoria shoots me a look.

Arturo chuckles loudly like a donkey.

"Yep! Play on Facebook is how I wrote it in on my business card."

Leo stands up. "Elena, *cara*, would you like to dance?" He extends his hand.

I grab it and join him on the dance floor. Michael Bublé's sultry "Feeling Good" tune is playing, and we dance pressed together.

It's obvious all eyes are on us since we're the only people on the dance floor.

Leo runs his hand down my back, and squeezes my ass. In this moment, no one else exists to me. In the past I'd never let a man touch me like this in public, in front of all the glaring eyes, but with Leo I'm glad he can't keep his hands off me.

I want him to crave me just as I crave him.

I kiss his cheek and whisper in his ear, "You are the sexiest thing I've ever seen, and I can't wait to get you in my bed."

Leo nibbles on my ear. "I want to leave this party and rip your dress off. I want you naked."

We sway together to the beat.

"Leo, I can't wait to have your hot tongue licking every inch of me."

"After I lick every inch of you ... then what?"

Maybe it's this sexy song that's taking over us.

"Then," I blush thinking about what I'm going to say, "I want you to stick your cock inside my pussy and pump your hips

into me until we come together, screaming in pleasure."

The wild woman is back.

The song ends, and before we can head back to our table, Leo leads us toward the bar. He orders two shots of tequila and hands me one.

"Shots?" I hold the glass in my hand. "I didn't know Mr. Beautiful likes to take shots."

"When Mr. Beautiful's girlfriend is rubbing up against him and saying dirty things in his ear, he needs to take a shot to calm his nerves."

I laugh at his confession. Here goes nothing. I down my shot, slowly licking the rim with my tongue as my eyes gaze into his.

He lets out a hiss of breath and takes his shot.

"We need to leave ... *pronto*." Leo slams his shot glass down on the bar.

"Leave?" Rosalie approaches us. "You haven't even shared a dance with your mama. How can you already be talking about leaving?"

"I think it would be lovely to see you dance with your mother," I say, looking at Leo with Rosalie. Teasing him when he's clearly in need of something from me. And only me.

And I have to admit, it's nice to see them next to each other. I can see their resemblance—they both have striking emerald eyes and dark brown hair. Rosalie looks young for her age as well.

"*Grazie*, Elena, for giving me a minute of my own son's time."

Another diss? Am I reading too much into this?

I scan Leo's eyes, but they seem to just be staring between Rosalie and myself.

"Okay, mama, let's dance." Leo takes his mother's hand and they walk out to the dance floor together.

They look adorable dancing and talking to one another. Rosalie softens her harsh personality when she's with Leo alone.

Staring at them, I daydream about my own family. I miss my parents and my siblings. I really have a great family, and it makes me a little sad to think of Leo growing up without a dad and with a mom who was depressed.

I want to wrap my arms around him and cuddle him like a big teddy bear. The need to protect him fills my heart.

"Elena, your boyfriend is on the dance floor. You shouldn't be standing here by yourself. Care for a dance?" Danilo asks me.

"Your wife won't mind?" I ask.

"No, she's dancing right now with our family friend."

I spot Gianna on the dance floor. She waves to me and smiles.

The song changes to a more upbeat tune. As I let loose with Danilo and the rest of the guests, I see Leo and Rosalie walk off the dance floor out of the corner of my eye.

Before the next song starts, I excuse myself from the dance floor to look for my dreamy boyfriend. I don't see him anywhere in the giant ballroom. Now seems like the perfect time to freshen up in the little girl's room.

On my way to the bathroom, Leo's voice halts my step.

He's loud tone startles me.

Walking toward the closed off room, I don't mean to eavesdrop, yet again, but if Leo is upset, I want to defend him or be by his side.

"Leonardo, I understand that she's cute and you want to just stay in bed all day, but she is not cut out to be *Signora Forte*."

You'd like a sentiment like that would belong to Victoria but that is Rosalie's voice. So much for making a great impression with his mom —guess not.

Leo's voice is louder than I've ever heard. "You have no idea what you are talking about. Elena would make an amazing Mrs. Forte. She makes me a better person."

My heart beats faster as I listen.

"Better person?" Rosalie laughs. "There's nothing wrong with you that this American girl can fix. You run one of the most important companies in this country, soon to be the world. *You* are on the cover of magazines, *you* make very important decisions daily, and *you* are the heir of two giant family fortunes." There's a long pause. "What will a 'social media' girl who works in a coffee shop do to better you? You are better than this! Better than her."

My hands clench into fists at my side.

Again with this bullshit. I can't believe how many people in Leo's life don't want us to be together for the fact that I am not "good enough" for him.

They don't even know a thing about me. I should barge in and tell her a little about my background, but I decide that she's not even good enough to know.

If she doesn't like me for what she's seen already I have no reason to tell her I own a multi-million dollar company and make important decisions daily.

"I don't want to hear this anymore. Elena is the best thing to happen to me. I love her and I will not have anyone in my life who won't accept our relationship ... even you."

He loves me?

He's defending me! My heart melts at his confession and the fact that he is fighting for not only me, but for us.

I see the door handle turn and I sprint into the bathroom.

Taking a good, hard look at myself in the mirror, I notice the glow on my face. Yes, Leo just got into a fight with his mother and Rosalie just said a whole bunch of nasty things about me, but I don't care. Leo loves me!

The man who didn't believe in love, or even marriage, mentioned both in that conversation.

Someone opens the bathroom door just as I decide to duck into a stall for a moment of privacy.

That's when my feelings of bliss are struck with contract.

Victoria and Rosalie are in the bathroom too.

"He says he *loves* her," Rosalie says. "I don't understand what she's doing to him. I'm worried."

I'm spying through the crack in the stall. They are both throwing their hands and arms in the air with dramatic force.

"Loves her?" Victoria fakes a gagging sound. "Leo is not capable of love! He has never loved anyone. Does she have something on him that we don't know?"

"I don't know how she'd be capable of that. She's not only poor but she doesn't seem bright either," Rosalie says.

Poor?

Stupid?

Let's add those to the list with 'trashy American.'

"I wouldn't be worried, Rosalie. Just like the girls in the past, he will get tired of her, and she will be kicked to the curb like the rest of Leo's discards." Victoria reapplies her lipstick in the mirror. "He's just wasting his time right now until he's ready to officially settle down with someone worthy of him."

Worthy? Does she think that's her? Get real.

"I trust you, Victoria. Don't let my Leonardo ruin his life with that tramp. She needs to go. Make it happen, now."

They leave the bathroom, and I walk out of the stall with my shoulders slumped.

Looking at myself in the mirror, gone is the glow from my complexion. Now I'm rather pale. Tears are about to spill from my eyes. Before my eyes can shed those tears, my phone vibrate in my clutch with a text message.

"What's up hooker? Miss you! xoxo Sophie"

Thank god. Just who I need to hear from in my time of freak out. I shoot her a quick text back.

"Funny story, I was just called that!"

"Say what? No one is allowed to call you a hooker but your BFF, I'm an exception to every rule."

Her reply comes in quick.

"It gets better ... it was by Leo's MOM!"

. . .

"Omg! Are you kidding me? I'm getting on the next flight to Italy to kick some old lady ass. Why did she call you that?"

"I overheard her talking with another girl who hates me. She also said I wasn't good enough for Leo."

"You better not be believing any of this garbage."

"I don't know, Soph. What if she has a point? What if I can't live up to all that a man like Leo needs me to be?"

"Elena, you are out of your mind! You are the kindest, smartest, funniest chick I know. You are the first to lend a hand or a hug. You come from a loving family. You are a hard worker. You should come clean about who you are to these bitches!"

"No girl, I told you I was keeping all of that under wraps when I was coming here. I need a break from being 'CEO Elena Scott,' it was getting to be too much. They should approve of me just as I am."

I read her kind text a few times to boost my ego. Best friends know just the right words to calm your nerves.

Leo says he loves me, and the fact that he defended me in front of his mother is admirable to me. I've never heard a man say such kind things about me.

I've also never had anyone fight for me. But my heart can't get around the fact and over and over again I'm reminded by the people in his life that I'm not good enough for him.

What do they need me to be?

I know Sophie says I should tell them I'm not who they think. But you know what? Who cares if I was! If they can't love me for who I am right now and how I make their son feel, why should I tell them anything different? My head feels like it's going to burst with all these questions spinning around inside.

Before I can ask myself any more self defeating questions, I run to the toilet and throw up.

———

I find Leo waiting for me at our table talking to Danilo and Gianna. He looks up from his conversation and his face pales.

"Elena, are you okay?"

"I'm fine. I just feel a little under the weather. I don't mean to do this to you and your mom, but I need to go."

"I'll text Mateo and have him bring the limo around to pick us up in the back so we can avoid the red carpet."

Leo engulfs me into a tight embrace.

This is my safe place.

The tears start to well up again but I do my best to fight them back and nuzzle into his chest. He holds me tighter than he normally does.

Leo's phone buzzes, and Mateo lets us know he's ready for us to come out. We say our goodbyes to Danilo and Gianna.

Leo doesn't even scan the crowd to look for his mother; he takes my hand and escorts me to the back of the ballroom so we can slip into the limo undetected.

I curl up into Leo's lap, getting as close to him as I possibly can, and we ride back to his place in silence.

It might be quiet in the car, but the doubts swirling around my mind are louder than life.

19

Practically bolting out of the limo, I nearly trip on the cobblestone driveway.

What's with Italy having all these fucking cobblestones?

Once inside Leo's home, I high tail it to his master bathroom and lock the door behind me.

I need a minute to myself to collect my thoughts after this whirl-wind night.

"Elena, are you okay?" Leo's voice carries through the door.

"I'm okay." I splash some cold water on my face. "I'll be out in just a minute."

What am I going to do? I can run out again like I did my first time here, but that's not fair to Leo. He deserves an explanation of why I need to leave. I love Leo with all my heart but I want to do what's right for him and his future.

Taking a long, hard look at myself in the mirror, I know what I need to do.

Walking out of the bathroom, I notice the bedroom is empty.

My overnight bag is near the door, which gives me a completely different idea.

Ruffling through the bag, I grab my sexiest lingerie and head back into the bathroom to change. I wanted this to be a special weekend for us both and I'm still going through with my original plan—play seductress.

I slip on a black silk, ultra low babydoll slip. It's cut low in a V shape that goes down to my belly, lined with ruffles and lace. Paired with the slip is a black lacy v-string panty. Everything is on display because the outfit is sheer. I leave my high heels on and, just as I'm about to open the door, I hear Leo making noise in the bedroom. He's back!

Leo is the kind of man who always takes control, no matter what the situation. It's unbelievably sexy, but tonight I'm going to be the one in charge.

Control is exactly what I crave.

I open the bathroom door, and Leo looks up from where he's sitting on the edge of the bed typing on his phone. He takes in a harsh breath and puts his phone down. He hasn't taken his eyes off me once.

Standing in the doorframe in what I hope is a sexy stance, I give him my best pinup girl pout. The way he's staring at me turns me on, and I can't help it, I giggle.

"Elena, I'm going to fucking ravage you."

Maybe the idea was better than I thought! Leo stalks toward me, but I meet at the bed quicker and shove him on top of it.

"I'm in charge tonight, Mr. Beautiful. Don't even think about taking control."

His emerald eyes darken—burning with desire.

"I'm all yours, *bella*. Do what you want." Leo leans back on the bed.

I straddle his hips and practically push my cleavage into his face.

"Suck," I command. Through the sheer lingerie, he sucks on my breast. Closing my eyes, I enjoy the pleasure tingling through me. "Enough."

He stops.

Starting at his neck, I slowly unbutton his dress shirt while crawling down his body.

His eyes never leave the sight of my breasts on display.

When I've gotten through all the buttons, I slip off his shirt and run my fingernails down his rock hard chest and ridiculously hot six pack.

My fingers make their way greedily toward his belt. I have it off in an instant, as well as his pants and boxer briefs.

Standing over him, I admire his body. I can't believe this guy is all mine for now.

She'll be kicked to the curb with the rest of his discards.

Victoria's nasty words try to throw me off my game but I bat them away.

No one is allowed to ruin this moment for us. I want to remember this forever.

Leo sits up but I push him back down and resume my straddle. His large hands rub up and down my thighs.

"No way, Jose. Don't you understand you aren't in control here? Now do as I say, lover boy," I command with a little laugh as I push his hands above his head.

With one hand holding his arms, I suck on his earlobes. I work my way down his neck, chest and stomach, trailing kisses, bites, and licks. He lets out a few low moans.

He tenses as I take his cock in my hands and stroke his length. I don't think I'll ever get over how big he is. I drop my hands to the side and instead place his dick in between my breasts, pushing them together as I rub him up and down.

When he looks ravished for more, I lean over him and rub my sex against him. I stop the rubbing because my body is willing to surrender to him too soon.

I don't want him to orgasm yet; I'm not ready to end this moment. I stand up toward the edge of the bed. Leo's eyes never leave my body.

He watches as I slip my hand into my panties and rub my own clit. His breath hisses between clenched teeth. I'm pushing him to the edge. I lock eyes with him and circle my bud with my fingers until I feel a dampness between my legs. I slip a finger inside myself, tilt my head back and let out a soft moan.

"Elena, if you don't stop, I'm going to come. Get back over here." Leo pulls me down on the bed and straddles me. His body is everywhere! He rips off my panties and slips his fingers inside my sex where my own fingers just were.

As he pushes his fingers in and out of my pussy, he takes his mouth and bites hard on my nipples through the sheer lingerie.

My senses are heightened, and my body feels ready to explode.

"Oh my God, Leo. I need you inside of me right now," I plead as I grip his biceps and push myself into his hand.

"You'll always need me." He positions his cock at my entrance and locks eyes with me.

Leo mouth crashes down on mine. He swirl his tongue around my own. I can't take much more and I really don't want to orgasm without him. As our tongues are busy dancing, I push my hips up to meet his cock and rub against him, slick with our juices.

I think I've pushed him to his max, and the next thing I know, he's slamming into me.

This moment is what I've been waiting for.

Leo slips his cock out and then slams back down into me. I meet each of his thrusts with my own. My legs shake and I grab onto his back with all my might and dig my nails in, holding on for dear life.

As we continue to ride each other, I bite down on his shoulder to stop myself from screaming out in ecstasy.

"Elena, I'm going to come!"

I push into him and can feel his manhood pulse inside of me. He collapses onto my body, and together we climax. The scent of our lust is in the air. He stays on top of me as we catch our breath and then he slips out of my sex.

He lies back on the bed, and I curl into his side and stroke his broad chest. I feel both of our hearts beating loudly. That was the best sex I've ever had.

"That was heavenly. I think I like when you are in control, too."

I laugh at his confession, and we hold each other tightly as we drift to sleep.

20

<hr />

It's a warm and sunny Sunday afternoon as Leo and I walk the streets of Rome hand-in-hand. We blend in with all the tourists on their honeymoons. We spent the morning in bed together, making love three times. We could give these honeymooners a run for their money.

We are much more relaxed today, winding down from last night's chaotic ball.

As we walk through the streets looking in the different markets, I spot an issue of TMZ Italia with Leo and myself on the cover. My heart stops a little seeing myself on the covers of magazines, again.

Billionaire Leonardo Forte Brings American Girlfriend To Charity Ball

Pictures of us from the red carpet pack the cover. Scanning the article, I don't see any mention of who I am, except for 'American girlfriend.' I'm glad to see they haven't done their research ... yet.

Seeing pictures from that night brings back both conversations I overheard, and I know what I need to do. I've been debating this since our mind blowing evening making love— yes I said making love—don't judge me.

The magazine cover is a reminder of what I want to avoid.

"Leo, I need to talk to you." I stop walking at the corner of the street. Leo backtracks to stand beside me.

"Yes, *cara*. What's going on?" His oh so beautiful emerald eyes shine down on me.

He has no idea what is going to happen, but his look changes as he reads the seriousness in my expression.

"Leo, I love you." I grab his hands. "I know we've only known each other for a very short time but I feel like you are the only person I am completely comfortable around. You are my Trevi Fountain wish." I laugh at the ridiculous notion. "I wake up thinking about you and I feel lucky I spend each night with you." Diverting my eyes, I glance to the ground. "But you deserve much more than me."

"Elena ..." Leo speaks but I hold my index finger up to silence his pleas.

"You are Rome's most eligible bachelor, and I know you don't believe in marriage. But I've realized, through loving you, how much I do. Your family, the people of Italy, and your company deserve for you to be with someone who can stand by you and represent you like you deserve. That's not me and it's been made very clear to me by the people in your life.

"I don't understand." Leo pulls his hands away.

"I haven't been accepted since we started dating and I know it will only get harder for us. If this is just the beginning, I can only imagine what would be ahead. I can't do this anymore. I can't be with someone who I feel like less of a person with. I have to let you go to find the person you are meant to be with."

The tears roll down my face. I'm sure we look crazy standing on this street corner.

"Elena, I don't know where this is all coming from but I don't agree with anything you just said. That's all ridiculous. We've been through this before. You, and only you, are the one that I want. I need you standing by my side, and you do make me proud. I have never felt the way I feel about you toward anyone else."

I can barely look in his eyes. What I am doing is for his benefit, even though it breaks my heart into a million pieces. I have to let this man go because we are both going to get hurt in the long run.

"Leo, I can't be with you anymore. I won't be with you."

"Elena, you don't mean this. I can't be without you again. That was the worst time of my life, I will fall apart." He grabs onto my hands once more.

Through the tears I manage to get my hands out of his grasp.

"I have to go. Please leave me alone."

Running across the crowded street, I fight not to look back at Leo who I left standing on the corner.

I hear the paparazzi before I see them. They must have just noticed their prince.

The loud shouting begins, "Leo! Leo! Leo!"

Flashes go crazy.

Turning to look back one last time at the man who has my heart, I see in the crowd of photographers one man wearing all black. He's not carrying a camera, and he's not shouting for Leo's attention. A mask covers all but his eyes.

And that's when I notice the gun.

Panic races through my body. Leo is blocking his face from the paparazzi, completely unaware of the gunman.

The man in black lifts his gun and points it right in the direction of Leo. Before I can think twice, I sprint across the street. I've never run so fast in my entire life.

"No!" I scream.

A loud shot rings out.

Jumping into Leo, I knock his large frame to the ground, landing directly on top of him.

The last thing I remember is looking into those emerald eyes and whispering, "I love you."

Pain consumes me and I pass out.

AFTERWORD

Ready for book 2 in the Eternal City Love series?

Leo & Elena are waiting for you! Pick up your copy of *Fighting For Mr. Beautiful* today.

Don't forget, reviews make the world a better place and I would be overjoyed if you left me one! <3 I'm forever grateful for each and every one of you who've taken the time to read this book.

And don't forget to sign up for my online newsletter. You'll get immediate updates on releases and exclusive sneak peeks.

ABOUT THE AUTHOR

CATERINA WANTS TO HEAR FROM YOU

To visit Caterina's website & subscribe to her email list, head to
http://www.caterinapassarellibooks.com

STAY SOCIAL
Find Caterina on her Facebook page at:
http://www.facebook.com/catpassarelli

Instagram:
http://www.instagram.com/caterinapassarelli

TikTok:
http://www.tiktok.com/caterinapassarelli

ALSO BY CATERINA PASSARELLI

The Eternal City Love Duet

My Mr. Beautiful
Fighting For Mr. Beautiful

The Signs Series

Fortunate Encounters
Encounters In Disguise
^Leo and Elena also show up in this novel

Contemporary Standalones

The Power of Salvation
Thirty Dates Later

Made in United States
Orlando, FL
03 April 2022

16435761R00088